GW00669638

Murder in Paris

A LOTTIE SPRIGG MYSTERY BOOK 2

MARTHA BOND

ISBN 978-1-7396766-4-3

marthabond.com

Lottie Sprigg Travels Mystery Series

~

Murder in Venice
Murder in Paris
Murder in Cairo
Murder in Monaco
Murder in Vienna

Murder in Paris

'I DON'T KNOW how Rosie managed it!' said Mrs Moore. 'She slipped her collar and off she went!'

Lottie Sprigg stared with dismay at the lead in her employer's hand. Rosie's collar dangled on the end, swaying gently in the blossom-scented breeze.

They stood in the Jardin des Tuileries, a beautifully landscaped park which stretched from the palatial Louvre Museum to the Place de la Concorde in the centre of Paris. Around them, Parisians and tourists were enjoying a sunny, springtime afternoon. Children played while their nannies watched from the shade of benches beneath the trees. Ladies promenaded in fashionable frocks and smart-suited men in boater hats accompanied them.

'Which way did she go?' asked Lottie, frantically scanning the wide, tree-lined pathways which stretched almost as far as she could see. There was no sign of her plump Pembroke Welsh Corgi.

'That way,' said Mrs Moore, pointing towards the Louvre. 'I would've gone after her, but thought I'd wait for you. Otherwise you'd have lost both of us!'

Lottie strode off, calling Rosie's name. Her heart pounded in her chest. Rosie couldn't have got far, could she? Surely no harm could come to her?

'Wait!' Mrs Moore caught up with her, puffing as she went. 'I'll take my parasol from you and you take Rosie's lead.'

If only Mrs Moore hadn't sent me back to the hotel for her parasol, thought Lottie. *None of this would have happened!*

'What made her run off?' she asked her employer as they marched towards the Louvre.

'I don't know. We've just been cooped up on an overnight train, haven't we? I expect she's relieved to be out in the fresh air again.'

Lottie and Mrs Moore had arrived that morning from Venice with an unscheduled stop in Milan. Their arrival had been filled with excitement as they'd explored the elegant hotel and ventured out for an afternoon walk in the sun. But now Lottie's stomach felt tied up in knots as she worried about Rosie lost in a strange city.

'Slow down a bit,' said Mrs Moore. 'I can't keep up, I've only got little legs.'

Lottie waited for her employer to join her. Mrs Moore wasn't wearing the most suitable clothes to move quickly in: a long burgundy skirt, a high-collared blouse and a woollen burgundy overcoat and fur stole. Her fashion tastes belonged to the Edwardian age, and she was quite content with that. Lottie wore her simple travelling clothes: a pleated skirt, cotton blouse and a light overcoat.

She hadn't owned Rosie for long, she'd adopted her in Venice after the dog lost her previous owner. They'd got on well during their short time together and Rosie had never run away before. So why had she done it now?

They reached a circular pond where water gushed sooth-ingly from a fountain in the centre. People sat on chairs and read newspapers, dozed and chatted. A man was painting the scene on an easel, Lottie would have stopped to admire the picture if she hadn't been worrying about Rosie. She was light-headed with worry and her mouth felt dry.

'I can't see her in the water,' said Mrs Moore, peering at the pond through her lorgnette. 'Does she like to swim?'

'I don't know. Should we go left, right or straight on? Which way do you think she went?'

'I really don't know. But don't worry, Lottie, I'm sure she's fine. She'll just be enjoying a frolic somewhere.'

Lottie took a deep breath. Her employer was probably right, but it was difficult to feel reassured. They turned left and continued along a path flanked by boxed shrubs and statues.

'There's a lamppost,' said Mrs Moore, pointing at an ornate example which was painted shiny black. 'Dogs like lampposts, don't they? She could be sniffing around one of those.'

'Let's keep looking,' said Lottie.

'I shall mention this in my next letter to my sister,' said Mrs Moore. 'I'm sure she'll be entertained by a tale of trying to find a lost dog in Paris!'

Mrs Moore was a wealthy American heiress and her sister was Lady Buckley-Phipps. Until a month ago, Lottie had worked as a maid for the Buckley-Phipps family at their large country house in Shropshire, England. She'd been overjoyed when Mrs Moore had employed her as a travelling companion. At nineteen years old, she was now travelling to places which most girls of humble birth could only dream of.

'What's going on over there?' said Mrs Moore. Lottie turned to see her employer training her lorgnette on an expanse of immaculate grass. 'Is that Rosie? Who's she with?'

In the centre of the lawn, two dogs scampered around each other in excitable circles.

Lottie's heart leapt with joy. 'It's her!'

'Now wait, we're not allowed on the grass, are we?'

'No. Oh dear.' Lottie paused at the edge of the lawn. 'The dogs shouldn't be there. Rosie!' She called out as loudly as possible, but Rosie chose not to hear. She called a few more times, but to no avail.

'Where's the owner of the other dog?' Lottie looked about, but the owner wasn't obvious. Turning back to the lawn, she realised she'd have to fetch Rosie herself. 'If I step onto the grass, I'll probably get told off by a park keeper.'

'Oh, they're not around at the moment. You'll be fine.'

'Alright then.'

Lottie removed her coat, handed it to Mrs Moore, then took the lead and collar and dashed off across the grass. As she neared the two dogs, she saw Rosie's friend was a little black terrier.

Both dogs continued to ignore her until she was able to grab hold of Rosie and put her collar back on.

'You don't know how worried I've been!' She bent down to give the dog a cuddle. 'You mustn't do that again!' Rosie gave her an appreciative lick, then turned back to her new friend. Lottie tugged on the lead and tried to persuade her to come with her.

'Oi!' came a shout from behind her.

A park keeper in blue uniform and a blue cap shouted and gesticulated from the pathway.

'Now we're in trouble, Rosie.' She gave a tug on the lead, but the corgi dug her paws into the grass. With a sigh, Lottie picked her up and carried her back to the path. The terrier followed at her heels.

'Not allowed!' shouted the park keeper. 'No one is allowed on the grass!'

'I'm sorry,' Lottie replied in French. 'I had to fetch my dog. I won't do it again.'

She returned to Mrs Moore and placed Rosie by her feet.

'I forgot you speak French, Lottie,' said her employer. 'Who'd have thought you could receive a good education in an orphanage?'

'I don't think it was a good education, only Miss Beaufort the schoolmistress who was French and insisted speaking to us in her own language. It was frustrating at the time but I'm grateful now.'

'And so am I! You can be my little translator while we're here.'

'Edmond!' A plump lady in a lilac low-waisted dress pounced on the terrier and attached a lead to its collar. She admonished him in French, then noticed Mrs Moore and gave her a puzzled glance. 'Roberta?'

Mrs Moore startled. 'Who? What? Oh my goodness! Harriet?'

'Yes! Now do tell me you were planning to call on me while you were in Paris?'

'Yes! Wasn't I just saying earlier, Lottie, that I would call on my dear old friend Harriet Lenoir while we were in Paris?'

'Yes,' lied Lottie.

'Well, I found you first!' Harriet Lenoir wore a lilac cloche hat over her fair, bobbed hair. She had a freckled complexion, an upturned nose, and looked about fifty - a similar age to Mrs Moore. 'When did I last see you? I think it was at your sister's place, Fortescue Manor, wasn't it?'

'Yes, it was. A good few years ago. This is my assistant Lottie Sprigg, she used to work at Fortescue Manor.'

Harriet Lenoir turned to Lottie with a smile. 'It's a pleasure to meet you.'

'Harriet is a friend of my sister's,' Mrs Moore explained to Lottie.

'I think I recall you visiting Fortescue Manor,' Lottie said to Mrs Lenoir.

'It's a delightful place. My husband and I always enjoyed

our visits there. In fact, I haven't been since he died. I must get in touch again with your sister, Roberta, it's been such a busy year that I haven't found the time. Are you here with your husband?'

'No.'

'He's in America?'

'I guess so. He left me.'

'Gosh how awful!'

'He ran off with a dancer from Petoskey, a small town in Michigan. I didn't mind him running off, in fact the dancer did me a favour. We'd got quite fed up with each other and we're divorced now. I'm so sorry to hear your husband passed away. Antoine was his name, wasn't it?'

'Yes.' She gave a sniff. 'He had a seizure last summer, and that was the end of that.'

'How awful!'

'It's been quite difficult.' She forced a smile onto her face. 'You must meet us tomorrow! I'll plan a boat trip on the Seine for you.'

'There's no need to go to so much trouble.'

'It's no trouble at all and I'd like you to meet everyone. Madeleine is getting married next month.'

'Is she indeed? How wonderful.'

'She's marrying Jacques Marchand, his father is a politician standing for election as mayor of the 16th arrondissement this summer.'

'She's marrying well then.'

'Oh, extremely well.' Mrs Lenoir gave a proud smile. 'Well, I must take naughty Edmond home with me now. He ran off! He seems to like your dog, though.'

Lottie glanced down at the corgi and the terrier who sat side-by-side.

'See you at midday tomorrow on the pier by the Eiffel Tower,' said Mrs Lenoir. 'Au revoir!'

. . .

'GOLLY, she didn't leave us much choice in the matter, did she?' said Mrs Moore as they watched Mrs Lenoir's departing form. 'But a boat trip on the Seine sounds fun, don't you think?'

Chapter Two

'THERE'S one thing you can say about the Eiffel Tower, Lottie, you get a nasty crick in your neck looking up at it.'

It was almost midday the following day, and Lottie, Mrs Moore and Rosie stood on the left bank of the River Seine, ready for the boat trip with the Lenoir family. They gazed up at the famous iron structure towering over them.

'When can we go up it?' asked Lottie, shielding her eyes from the sun.

'*Go up it*? You won't catch me going up that.'

'But we can't visit Paris without going up the Eiffel Tower.'

'It will make me dizzy. And I don't want to be stranded up there feeling all dizzy.' Mrs Moore turned her back on the tower and surveyed the river. 'I suppose Harriet and her family will turn up in a moment. She's English, you know, although she's lived in Paris since the age of eighteen, I believe. She married a Frenchman and has been settled here ever since. It's very sad to hear he died last year. I hope she's not offended that I didn't tell her I would be in Paris, I wasn't planning to avoid her but I can't say I was desperate to see her either. People like

8

Harriet can make demands on your time, I find. And it's rather nice to have time to do what you please, isn't it? And it's important that I make Prince Manfred's acquaintance while we're here.'

Prince Manfred of Bavaria was the reason Mrs Moore had travelled to Paris. He was considered to be the most eligible bachelor in Europe, and Mrs Moore was hoping he would be her fourth husband. Having narrowly missed dancing with him at a ball in Venice, Mrs Moore was keen to meet him while in Paris. 'I expect Prince Manfred is staying at the Ritz, he usually does,' she said. 'And, as luck would have it, the Ritz is just a short walk from our hotel. Once we're finished on the boat, I shall write a little note to him explaining that we're here and then you can deliver it to his hotel, Lottie. I hope we can arrange at least one engagement with him, I don't want our trip to Paris to be wasted.'

'Roberta!' A lady in peachy-pink waved at them from a gleaming white boat with a polished timber cabin.

'Oh, there she is, let's go. Hopefully this won't take up too much of our day.'

ON BOARD THE BOAT, Rosie was greeted by Edmond the terrier and the pair skipped around each other. Lottie and Mrs Moore were introduced to Harriet Lenoir's daughter, Madeleine, her son Charles, and Madeleine's fiancé, Jacques Marchand.

Madeleine was similar in age to Lottie and looked like her mother: plump, with fair bobbed hair, a freckled face and upturned nose. She wore a low-waisted jade green dress with a wide collar and a matching hat.

Mrs Lenoir was keen to tell them her son, Charles, was training to be a solicitor. He was square-jawed and also had the Lenoir freckles and upturned nose. He looked a little older

9

than his sister and wore a smart beige suit and a boater hat. The trouser of his left leg was folded and pinned to his thigh and he leant on a pair of crutches for support. Lottie wondered if he had suffered the injury in the war.

Jacques was a round-faced young man with hooded blue eyes. He wore a dark suit with a silk tie, and a gold watch chain hung across his waistcoat, glinting in the sunshine.

Lottie wondered if the three young people were here against their will, they'd smiled only weakly as Harriet Lenoir had introduced them. 'We were due to be joined by Florence, Charles's fiancée,' said Mrs Lenoir. 'But she's not feeling well today. So it will just be the six of us.'

'Lovely,' said Mrs Moore.

They made themselves comfortable in an outside seating area at the back of the boat, glasses of champagne rested on a round silver tray on a little table. 'Take one everyone before they topple over!' said Mrs Lenoir. They did so as the white-uniformed skipper in the cabin started up the engine and steered the boat out into the middle of the river.

The damp breeze refreshed Lottie's face and whipped at her bobbed hair. She glanced around at the Eiffel Tower, the tree-lined river embankment and the elegant bridge which spanned the river. She was in Paris! It was thrilling to see such a famous city.

'Roberta is the daughter of a wealthy railway tycoon,' Harriet Lenoir explained to her family. 'She's from... where is it again, Roberta?'

'Pennsylvania.'

'That's right. We stayed with her sister, Lady Buckley-Phipps, when you were younger. Do you remember Fortescue Manor?'

'I think so,' said Charles. Madeleine nodded, seemingly underwhelmed.

'And Lottie was a maid before Roberta brought her on her

travels,' explained Mrs Lenoir. 'Isn't that nice of Roberta?' She turned to Lottie. 'Where are your family from?'

'I don't know.'

'You don't know?'

'Shropshire, possibly. That's where I grew up.'

'Lottie grew up in an orphanage,' said Mrs Moore.

'Goodness, really?'

Lottie felt her face warm up as everyone glanced at her sympathetically. 'I had a happy childhood,' she said, not wanting their pity. She turned away to look at the grand buildings overlooking the river with their tall windows and wrought-iron balconies.

'Where's this boat going?' Madeleine asked her mother. Like her brother, she spoke fluent English with a hint of a French accent.

'Around the Île de la Cité and back. Not far. Now don't look so ungracious, Maddy! It's fun to do these things. It's rare that we see the city from the river, isn't it? When you live in a place as beautiful as Paris, it's easy to fall into the trap of doing the same old things all the time. It's nice to do something different and see everything from a new perspective.'

'Wise words, Mother,' said Charles.

'Thank you, I like to think so.'

'Congratulations on your engagement, Madeleine,' said Mrs Moore. 'You must be awfully busy organising the wedding.'

Madeleine nodded.

'Oh, it's been terribly busy!' said Mrs Lenoir. 'There's so much to organise, isn't there, Maddy? We have yet another dress fitting tomorrow and there's been all manner of toing and froing with the caterers. I'm anxious about the menu, there are going to be a lot of important guests at the wedding and they have high expectations.'

'Probably not as high as you think,' said Madeleine, examining her nails.

'I know what their expectations are,' said Mrs Lenoir. 'And believe me, you'll thank me for making such an effort.'

'And what do you do, Monsieur Marchand?' Mrs Moore asked Jacques.

'I am a student of mathematics.'

'Oh.'

'My aim is to prove Fermat's Last Theorem.'

'Oh?'

'It's a puzzle which has endured for nearly three hundred years.'

'Gosh, that's a long time.'

'We're about to pass beneath the Pont Alexandre III!' said Mrs Lenoir. 'It commemorates the Russian tsar Alexander III. Isn't it beautiful?' The span of the bridge was covered with carved stone cherub faces, shells and foliage. Ornate lampposts ran along its length and gold statues stood on columns at either end. 'It looks like something out of a fairy tale doesn't it? And there in the centre are the nymphs of the River Seine.' She pointed to a statue of two scantily clothed women holding gold torches and supporting what appeared to be a coat of arms.

'Quite beautiful,' said Mrs Moore.

Rosie and Edmond continued to scamper about together, and Mrs Lenoir drained her champagne. 'So what are your plans while you're here in Paris, Roberta?'

'I'm hoping to rendezvous with an acquaintance of mine, Prince Manfred of Bavaria.'

Mrs Lenoir's eyes widened. 'Goodness, Roberta! I had no idea you kept such company!'

Mrs Moore gave a little laugh. 'Well, he's not company as such, not yet anyway. But he doesn't know I'm in Paris yet, so I shall have a message delivered to him later.'

'How enchanting! I should like to meet him.'

Mrs Moore's face stiffened. 'Everyone wants to meet him, he's very much in demand. Anyway, Harriet, I was telling Lottie a bit about you earlier. I remember you saying you came to Paris when you were eighteen, is that right?'

'Yes, it was my father's idea. We lived in Surrey and I was a clumsy little thing and not particularly pretty. I was more interested in riding ponies than anything else and always had dirt on my face or straw in my hair. My father despaired! So he sent me to live with his cousin here in Paris in the hope the city would refine me...' She paused, as if forgetting herself for a moment. Her brow furrowed momentarily, then she forced a smile. 'And here I've stayed ever since! Paris certainly refined me because I met the aspiring politician, Antoine Lenoir, and we fell in love and got married when I was twenty-six. Charles arrived the following year.'

'Twenty-five years ago,' said Madeleine. 'He's an old man now.'

'When Antoine and I met, it was love at first sight,' said Mrs Lenoir.

'Goodness, how romantic.'

'It was. Look, there's the Gare d'Orsay!' She pointed to a large, ornate building on the left bank. It had big, round windows and an enormous clock. 'Have you ever seen a railway station as beautiful as that?'

'I don't think I have,' said Mrs Moore. She turned to Jacques. 'I hear your father is standing for election as mayor of the 16th arrondissement.'

'Yes, that's right. And he'll win no problem at all,' said Jacques.

'Well, that's nice. Have you ever felt tempted to follow your father into politics?'

'Well, I would like to but my mother tells me I'm a talented mathematician, so I should concentrate on that instead. She says she couldn't cope with two politicians in the house!' He followed this with a guffawing laugh which made Lottie's teeth clench.

Mrs Moore moved the conversation on. 'I hope you don't mind me asking Charles, but were you injured in the war?'

'Yes, at the Battle of Amiens. At least the loss of my leg meant I could come home.'

'It could have been so much worse!' said Mrs Lenoir. 'But thankfully it wasn't. Such a worrying time for us all.'

'And when is your wedding, Charles?' asked Mrs Moore.

'We don't know yet. We're waiting to get Maddy's wedding out of the way before we decide.'

'Very sensible, isn't he?' said Mrs Lenoir. 'I couldn't cope with two weddings at the same time!'

'It's a shame not to meet your fiancée, Florence,' Mrs Moore said to Charles.

'There was never any danger of her coming,' said Madeleine. 'She doesn't like us!'

'That's enough, Maddy,' said Mrs Lenoir. 'Mrs Moore doesn't want to hear about petty disagreements. Now then, look ahead! Can you see Notre-Dame cathedral?'

The river had narrowed as they passed down one side of the Île de la Cité. Stone walls rose on either side of them and Lottie could see the two imposing towers of the ornate cathedral.

'Famed for its use of flying buttresses,' said Jacques.

'Oh Jacques, what are you talking about?' said Madeleine.

'Notre-Dame was one of the first Gothic cathedrals to be constructed with flying buttresses. Without them, the walls would fall outwards.'

'Well, that's very interesting indeed, Jacques,' said Mrs Moore.

'The buttresses allow for larger window size because the

walls don't need to bear so much of the load. With Chartres Cathedral they made the mistake of—'

'Jacques,' snapped Madeleine. 'Now is not the time for one of your lecture sessions. We're here to enjoy ourselves. Supposedly.'

'Which hotel are you staying at, Mrs Moore?' asked Charles.

'Le Meurice.'

'Very nice!' said Mrs Lenoir. 'And you're just around the corner from our apartment! That explains why we bumped into each other at the Jardin des Tuileries. We shall be able to see much more of you during your stay in Paris!'

Chapter Three

BACK AT THE HOTEL, Lottie and Mrs Moore tucked into afternoon tea. Their table was crowded with little china plates, silver cutlery, napkins and an elaborate three-tiered cake stand.

'I'm not sure what Madeleine Lenoir sees in Jacques Marchand,' said Mrs Moore. 'He's quite a bore, isn't he? I suppose he's from the right sort of family and the Lenoirs consider that to be important. Have you had one of the salmon sandwiches, Lottie? What are they like?'

'Very nice.' Lottie finished her mouthful and eyed one of the freshly baked scones.

'I'll pour the tea. The trouble with Harriet is that she always was a social climber. Her origins are quite humble but she likes to move in the right circles. I don't think she would have befriended my sister if she hadn't been married to a lord. Oh dear, this tea looks a little weak, doesn't it? Perhaps I should have left it to brew longer. I don't like leaving it too long though because there's nothing worse than stewed tea. Goodness, listen to me! I almost sound like a British person discussing tea now. Where was I? Oh yes, Harriet. I don't like to speak too harshly of her, though, as she was very generous taking us on the boat trip. Hopefully our social duty is done now, I can't say I want our time here to be monopolised by the Lenoirs, there are other things I'd like to do. Which reminds me! I must draft my letter to Prince Manfred.'

In Mrs Moore's hotel room, Lottie slumped on a plush velvet chair, having had her fill of sandwiches, scones and cakes. Rosie lay by her feet, tired from her frolics on the boat. Mrs Moore sat at the dressing table, a sheet of hotel letter paper in front of her and pen in hand.

'If I don't hurry up with this note, Prince Manfred will move elsewhere before I get the chance to meet with him. "Dear Prince Manfred,"' she narrated as she wrote. '"How delighted I was to see you at Signora Contarini's masquerade ball at the Palazzo Sacrati in Venice. It's a shame the tragic incident that night meant we couldn't share a dance." Oh dear, does that sound wrong? I sound like I'm more upset about the fact we couldn't dance together than the murder. I don't want to come across as too uncaring.'

She screwed up the letter, threw it into the wastepaper basket and began again on a new sheet. '"Dear Prince Manfred, it was delightful to meet you at Signora Contarini's masquerade ball in Venice, it's a terrible shame the evening was cut short and that we didn't find the time to dance together." Oh no that sounds just as bad.' She balled up the letter and discarded it. 'Perhaps I could be a little more playful in my wording? Prince Manfred has a good sense of fun, and I think I could make it a little less dry. "Dear Prince Manfred, how naughty of you to skip off to Paris without informing me! I had been hoping we would find an opportunity to spend time together in Venice and yet you left without notice." Oh no, that sounds rather yearning, doesn't it? Oh darn it, I don't think I'm ever going to get this letter right. Am I thinking about it too much, Lottie? Perhaps I'm trying too hard. I can't decide how long to make the letter. He's quite a jolly, sociable chap and would appreciate something chatty, I think. But he's also rather busy and I don't think he would have the time to read anything too long.'

'Why don't you just let him know that you're staying in Paris and look forward to meeting him while you're here?'

'That sounds quite sensible.'

IT WAS early evening by the time Lottie ventured out with the letter to be delivered to Prince Manfred at the Ritz Hotel. She took Rosie with her.

They walked along a wide boulevard with grand buildings four or five storeys high. Fashionable boutiques lined the street and Lottie admired the expensive coats, dresses, hats and shoes in the windows. Well-dressed ladies carried parasols and shopping bags, and Rosie enjoyed greeting some of their well-groomed dogs.

The street opened out into an expansive square, Place Vendome, where a tall column stood in the centre. Lottie was impressed by how wide and spacious this part of Paris felt, London's streets seemed narrow and crowded in comparison.

The Ritz occupied a corner of Place Vendome and was recognisable by its white awnings and the shiny cars parked outside. As Lottie approached the building, a lady dressed in furs was helped out of a car, then followed into the hotel by two footmen loaded down with shopping bags and hat boxes.

The hotel lobby felt grand and important. Lottie tried not to feel too intimidated by it and made her way past a large staircase and marble columns to a polished reception desk. She handed Prince Manfred's letter to a thin, pale-faced man with dark hair combed back from his tall forehead. She exchanged a few words in French with him, then left the hotel with a spring in her step, pleased she'd successfully delivered the letter.

It was a mild evening and an hour yet until sunset, so Lottie took Rosie for a little walk so they could see more of Paris. After a short stroll, they were on the wide, tree-lined Champs-Élysées where the famous Arc de Triomphe sat at the far end. Lottie turned into a narrower street where smart, aproned waiters loitered outside their restaurants, hoping to entice diners in. After a pleasant stroll through a little park, Lottie decided to head back to the hotel.

'Mrs Moore will be wondering where we've got to, Rosie.' She glanced around, wondering which way to go. 'The trouble is, I think we're lost.' She looked down at her dog. 'Can you remember the way?' Rosie returned her gaze with her large, dark eyes. 'No, I don't suppose you do.'

Lottie headed in the direction she thought was right and the street narrowed. The shops she passed now were smaller and functional: a bakery and a grocer's shop.

A young man on a delivery bicycle pedalled towards her along the road. He caught her eye, then hopped his bicycle onto the pavement. Although the move was deftly performed, he lost his balance and collided with the bakery window. He came off his bicycle, and it fell next to him, wheels spinning.

Lottie gasped and dashed over to him. 'Are you alright?' she asked in French. The young man muttered as he hauled himself up and rubbed his head.

'Pierre!' A man in a baker's cap and apron stormed out of the shop. 'What are you doing?' He glanced at Lottie. 'And what have I told you about showing off in front of the girls?'

Pierre's face reddened as he gave Lottie a sidelong glance and picked up his bicycle.

'You could have gone through the window!' said the baker. 'My customers don't want shards of glass in their bread!'

Pierre apologised, and the baker returned inside.

'I hope you're not hurt,' said Lottie.

'No, I'm fine.' He picked his cap off the floor and put it on his head. He was about the same age as Lottie and had dark hair which flopped into his green eyes.

'I wonder if you can help me?' she said. 'I think I'm lost.' He smiled as Lottie asked him for directions to the hotel.

'You're next to it,' he said.

'Am I?'

'Yes, the back of the hotel is just there.' He pointed to a building behind him.

'How silly of me, thank you.'

'You're not silly. You speak good French.'

Lottie felt her face heat up because he was quite handsome and he'd paid her a compliment.

She went on her way and tried to find a door at the back of the hotel. A young couple passed her, arm-in-arm. The woman wore a sequinned evening dress which skimmed her knees and a beaded headdress with a feather in it. Dark make-up shadowed her eyes and her lips were painted bright red. She was laughing with her companion, who wore a pale suit and a beret which was positioned on his head at a jaunty angle.

The woman caught Lottie's eye and there was a glimpse of recognition before she looked away and quickened her pace. Lottie watched the pair continue down the street.

'How interesting,' Lottie said to Rosie. 'I'm sure that was Madeleine Lenoir.'

Chapter Four

THE FOLLOWING day was taken up with shopping. 'I can't visit Paris without buying clothes,' said Mrs Moore. 'It would be extremely remiss of me. After all, we're in the city of fashion! It won't do you any harm to have a few new outfits either, Lottie. You need some smart things just in case we attend a high society event while we're here.'

Mrs Moore spent a small fortune in the fancy shops on the Champs-Élysées. She bought several new outfits for herself and a turquoise satin dress for Lottie, which had a fashionable low waist and pleated skirt. Lottie couldn't wait to wear it somewhere special.

During a break from the shops, they sat at a sunny table outside a cafe and sipped coffee. Mrs Moore observed the surroundings through her lorgnette. 'This is the life isn't it? Paris in the springtime! All the great and good going about their daily business.'

Mrs Moore was clearly enjoying Paris and Lottie liked it very much, too. She even felt slightly sophisticated as she picked up her delicate coffee cup and held her little finger out as she sipped from it.

'My father would have loved Paris,' said Mrs Moore. 'But he never made it here. He only crossed the Atlantic twice - to Liverpool and back. He swore he'd never make the journey again because he got such dreadful sea sickness.' She sipped her coffee. 'I miss him a lot. But at least I knew my father. I've often wondered what it's like to be an orphan. What's it like, Lottie?'

'I don't suppose I know any different. I grew up with other orphans, so I didn't think I was unusual until I went into service with your sister. Then I realised many people were brought up by their parents. I didn't feel too sad about it though because I was happy in the orphanage.'

'Do you ever wonder who your parents were?'

'Sometimes.' Lottie had been left as a baby on the doorstep of Oswestry Orphanage in Shropshire. She'd been swaddled in blankets and placed in a box. 'Miss Beaufort told me I'd been well looked after before I was left on the doorstep,' said Lottie. 'Apparently, I was clean and well-fed.'

'That's something, I suppose. I can only imagine your mother struggled to look after you. Perhaps she was too poor, or you were born out of wedlock. Your mother may have been a maid who got into trouble with the master of the house or his son. It happens quite frequently.'

Lottie had often wondered who her parents were. As a girl, she'd dreamed she was the secret child of a king and queen who would turn up one day and take her to live with them in their palace. She realised the scenarios Mrs Moore had in mind were more likely, but she could still dream.

'Perhaps your parents died,' said Mrs Moore. 'Oh no, don't look so glum, Lottie! I'm sorry, I said that without thinking. I shall cheer us up by ordering some crêpes. Waiter!'

. . .

THERE WAS a letter waiting for Mrs Moore at the reception desk when they returned to the hotel. She eagerly ripped open the envelope before they'd even got to her room.

'Oh, it's from Harriet,' she said, the disappointment evident in her voice. 'She wants us to dine with them this evening. We only saw them yesterday, didn't we? I'm not sure I want to go, I'm worried she'll bore us about the wedding. And as for that fiancé of Madeleine's... I think he'll just bore us to tears!'

'Maybe he has an interesting side to him?'

'I hope so. Otherwise Madeleine is doomed.'

Lottie wondered if she should tell Mrs Moore that she'd seen Madeleine with another man. Although she'd been quite certain it was Madeleine, there was a risk she'd been mistaken. There was also a risk that Mrs Moore would tell Harriet Lenoir about it. Lottie decided to remain quiet on the matter, telling herself it was Madeleine's business and not hers.

The telephone by Mrs Moore's bed rang. Lottie answered, and the receptionist told her that a messenger boy was waiting in reception for Mrs Moore.

'That will be Prince Manfred's reply!' said her employer. 'I wonder what he's said? How exciting! Please go and fetch it for me, Lottie.'

Lottie did so, and was surprised to discover the message was being delivered by Pierre the delivery boy who'd fallen off his bicycle the previous evening. He had a bruise on his cheek. 'It's nice to see you again,' he said with a smile. 'And unexpected. I've been sent here with a message.' His brow furrowed. 'Although you're not Mrs Moore, are you?'

'No, I'm her assistant Miss Lottie Sprigg.'

'It's nice to meet you, Miss Sprigg. I'm Pierre Renard.' He took off his cap and gave a little bow.

'I already know your name is Pierre.'

'How?'

'Because the baker shouted at you.'

He gave an embarrassed laugh. 'Anyway, Mrs Lenoir sent me.'

'Not Prince Manfred?'

'No, who's he?'

'Someone Mrs Moore is expecting a message from. She's already received a letter from Mrs Lenoir today, do you have another one?'

'No, she sent me here for Mrs Moore's reply. She wants to know if Mrs Moore accepts her invitation to dinner this evening.'

'I had better ask her.'

Lottie asked to use the receptionist's telephone and called Mrs Moore's room.

'Yes hello? Bonjour, I mean. Who's this?'

'Mrs Moore, it's Lottie. Mrs Lenoir is requesting a reply to her dinner invitation.'

'She's in reception?'

'No, she sent the messenger boy.'

'Goodness, the woman's impatient, isn't she? I was delaying my reply because I wanted to see if Prince Manfred would extend an invitation. But as I've heard nothing from him, then I suppose we'll have to accept.'

Lottie replaced the telephone receiver. 'Mrs Moore would be delighted to attend,' she said to Pierre.

'Excellent.' He smiled and replaced his cap. 'I shall see you around.'

THE LENOIR FAMILY lived in an attractive apartment building on a quiet street about a ten-minute walk from Lottie and Mrs Moore's hotel. A tall, stooped man in a dark blue suit answered the door. His face was lined and he had a head of scruffy grey hair.

'Who are you here to see?' he asked in French.

'The Lenoir family,' replied Lottie.

'You're British!' he said in English. 'I like British people.'

'I'm American,' said Mrs Moore.

'I like American people too! Parisians say their city is overrun with foreigners these days, but I like foreigners. They make the place interesting. Imagine if Paris was only full of French people? That would be boring, wouldn't it? And you have a friendly dog too.' He patted Rosie on the head. 'Is the dog British or American?'

'She's Italian.'

'Even better! I love Italian dogs, they're my favourite dogs.'

Rosie looked pleased, as if she'd understood him. He showed them into a large echoey lobby with a tiled floor and a wide staircase at the far end.

'Now, what are your names? I need to make sure Mrs Lenoir is expecting you.' He walked over to a table with a book on it. 'She's very particular about her guests, I've heard. In fact, you're very lucky to be invited here at all, she doesn't extend dinner invitations to just anybody you know.'

'We must be very privileged in that case,' said Mrs Moore and gave him their names.

He wrote them down in the book. 'Wonderful American and British names.'

'Do you flatter all your visitors in this manner?'

'No, I'm rude to most of them.'

Mrs Moore laughed. 'I bet you're not, really.'

'Oh, I am.'

'May I ask your name?' Mrs Moore seemed quite taken with him.

'Lucien Boucher.'

'Well, we shall tell our hostess this evening what a delightful concierge she has.'

'I'm not a concierge, I'm the gardien.'

'The guardian?'

'Gardien, it sounds slightly different.'

'Does it? My apologies for not getting it quite right.'

'No need to apologise. And please tell Mrs Lenoir how good I am. I'm trying to do my best, I've only been working here for two weeks.'

'Two weeks? But you seem to know what you're doing.'

'Of course, it's not a difficult job. I live in a little apartment here.' He pointed to a door next to the staircase. 'And I keep an eye on everything. I fix broken things, clean things and greet the visitors. I write their names down in this visitor's book.'

'An important job.'

'Very important.' He grinned.

'Where did you work before?' asked Mrs Moore.

'I did a similar job, but not in Paris, in Rouen in Normandy.'

'Lovely.'

'Not lovely, it was boring. I'm actually Parisian, I was born in this city and lived here until my twenties. Then my wife left me and I moved away to recover from my broken heart.'

'Oh poor you, Mr Boucher!'

'Thank you for the sympathy, it is most appreciated.'

'Did you marry again?'

'No. In fact we never divorced.'

'Did you not? Golly.'

'It costs a lot of money.' He smiled. 'Anyway, I'm happy to be back in Paris where I can speak to delightful Americans like yourself, Mrs Moore.'

She laughed again. 'Now I think you're flattering me too much.'

'Am I? I'm sorry. I get a little carried away sometimes. Now what have you seen of Paris so far?'

'We've been on a boat trip.'

'Very nice. What else?'

'That's about all.'

'I'd like to go up the Eiffel Tower,' said Lottie.

'And I don't,' said Mrs Moore.

'You must see Montmartre!' said Mr Boucher. 'It's my favourite part of Paris. You'll love the charming little streets. It's on a hill so you can see wonderful views of the city. You must visit Sacré-Cœur Basilica while you're there, it's a beautiful church.'

'Well that sounds quite delightful,' said Mrs Moore. 'Thank you for the tip, Mr Boucher.'

'I am always happy to help.' He grinned. 'I mustn't delay you any longer, Madame Lenoir will be waiting. Her family occupies two floors of this building, the main entrance to their apartment is on the third floor.'

. . .

HARRIET LENOIR WAS DRESSED in floaty silk of sapphire blue. She received Lottie and Mrs Moore in her fourth-floor drawing room with tall windows overlooking the street. The room was furnished in white and gold and was filled with elegant furniture and expensive looking ornaments.

'Well, this is very nice, Harriet,' said Mrs Moore. She surveyed the room through her lorgnette. 'You must have quite a few valuables in here.'

'A few.'

'Any prized possessions?'

'I'm rather fond of the clock,' she pointed to the mantel-piece and an elaborate gold and porcelain clock topped with an ornamental urn. 'It has two matching candelabras.'

'So it has.' Mrs Moore admired the display. 'Quite exquisite.'

Charles Lenoir entered the room, supported by his crutches.

'Good evening Charles!' said Mrs Moore. 'Your mother is just showing us her ornaments.'

He rolled his eyes. 'Fussy old things which collect the dust.'

'Charles is modern in his tastes,' said Mrs Lenoir. 'He thinks my ornaments are all very old-fashioned. Even though some of them are extremely valuable!'

'I like this lamp,' said Mrs Moore, pointing to a gold, fringed lampshade on a table by the fireplace.

'Quite inexpensive, I'm afraid, but I have it in here because I like the colour. The base is green onyx.'

'Not marble?'

'No, although it looks like marble doesn't it? Now the two lamps on that sideboard are marble and quite valuable.' She pointed to a pair of white and gold lamps with bases shaped like urns on plinths. 'They're Victorian and cost quite a bit back then. They're the most expensive items in the room.'

'Really? Even more than the table?'

'Yes!' Mrs Lenoir gave a little laugh. 'Funny, isn't it?'

Edmond the terrier scampered into the room and Rosie dashed over to him, tail wagging. Lottie welcomed the distraction, the conversation about valuable ornaments was boring her.

Charles seemed bored, too. He sat in a chair by the fireplace and attempted to stifle a yawn.

'Where have Maddy and Jacques got to?' said Mrs Lenoir. 'We can't have our champagne until they arrive.'

'Can't we?' said Mrs Moore. 'That's a shame.'

'I'll go and see where they are.' Mrs Lenoir left the room.

'Is your fiancée Florence still unwell?' Mrs Moore asked Charles.

'She is. And...' He rubbed his brow. 'Although I shouldn't really air our family grievances, it's probably best you know that Florence doesn't get along well with my sister and Jacques.'

'That's a shame. Families can be complicated, can't they?'

'They can. We have the complication of Florence having formerly been engaged to Mr Marchand.'

'No!' Mrs Moore's jaw dropped. 'Really?'

'Yes. Florence ended the engagement and my sister doesn't like her as a result. Perhaps Maddy worries that Jacques still has some affection for her. It doesn't bother me, it's quite forgotten about as far as I'm concerned. But Maddy can be awkward about it.'

'Thank you for being so frank with us Charles, it helps to be aware of such matters.'

'Like I say, it doesn't bother me. Although Jacques was rather beastly to Florence.'

'Really? I hope he doesn't do the same to your sister.'

'He won't. It was all to do with the cats.'

'Cats?'

'Florence adores cats and has half a dozen of them. Jacques hates cats and was frequently mean about them. It upset Florence a great deal and she put an end to things.'

'Understandably.'

'Oh dear, I hope I haven't put a dampener on the evening.'

'You haven't, Charles. Please don't worry about that.'

'Here they are!' said Mrs Lenoir, returning to the room with Madeleine and Jacques. 'I found them!'

The unsmiling couple followed her into the room. Madeleine wore a stylish blush pink dress and Jacques was dressed in a smart dark suit. As soon as Madeleine caught Lottie's eye, she glanced away again. She seemed to know Lottie had seen her with another man.

They consumed champagne and olives, then the bell rang for dinner. Mrs Lenoir led them downstairs to the tasteful dining room on the third floor. Rosie and Edmond scampered down after them. 'What a marvellous place,' said Mrs Moore. 'So much space and light! You don't get apartments like this in London. My Chelsea townhouse is quite poky in comparison.'

'London's often glorified,' said Mrs Lenoir. 'When really it's just cramped and smoky, and the streets are clogged up with motorcars. Perhaps you could make Paris your home, Roberta?'

'Well, there's a thought. Although it does rather depend.'

'On what?'

'On whether I secure myself a fourth husband.'

'Oh, the prince?'

'Well, that would be nice. I could happily live in a fairy tale castle on a hilltop in Bavaria.'

'I'm sure you could, Roberta. And I can imagine you in one too! In fact, I quite fancy the idea myself.'

'No, I think you have everything you need here in Paris.'

'Perhaps. Although the thought of marrying again hasn't escaped my mind.'

Lottie wondered if Mrs Lenoir was now considering Europe's most eligible bachelor as a potential match.

Onion soup was served in elegant bowls with lion head handles. This was followed by sea bass in a creamy sauce and a palate cleansing lemon sorbet. Lottie did her best to use the correct pieces of silver cutlery in the right order.

'How did the dress fitting go today, Madeleine?' asked Mrs Moore.

'It went fine, thank you.' The young woman's face remained sullen.

'It went more than fine, didn't it Maddy?' said Mrs Lenoir. 'It's almost perfect! Just a few minor adjustments are needed, and I think Jacques is going to be thrilled when he sees Madeleine on her wedding day. In fact, he'll barely recognise her!'

'I pay little attention to clothes,' said Jacques.

Charles choked on his wine as if stifling a laugh.

'But we're talking about a wedding dress, Jacques!' said Mrs Lenoir. 'Not just ordinary clothes!'

The young man shrugged. 'Wedding dresses all look the same to me.'

Madeleine's lips were pursed so tightly that her mouth had almost disappeared.

'Well, I love wedding dresses!' said Mrs Moore. 'So much so that I've worn three!'

'A proper wedding dress each time, Roberta?' asked Mrs Lenoir.

'Yes! I refuse to be one of those women who merely wear something ordinary at their subsequent weddings. A marriage should be properly celebrated! I suppose I'm quite unusual because I've married three times. Most people only marry once.'

A few seconds of silence followed then Madeleine spoke. 'I adore your enthusiasm for marriage, Mrs Moore. And I think Jacques needs to get a bit more excited about our wedding.'

'I am enthusiastic about the wedding,' he said. 'In fact, wait until you see my dancing!' He followed this with one of his guffawing laughs, which made Lottie's toes curl.

Chapter Six

FOR THE NEXT COURSE, they dined on duck à l'orange served with asparagus and dauphinoise potatoes. Lottie's stomach was full, and she wondered how many courses were left to come. She felt something brush against her foot and bent down to look beneath the table, she smiled when she saw Rosie and Edmond happily playing there.

'We had a pleasant conversation earlier with the concierge,' said Mrs Moore. 'Actually, he corrected me when I called him that. What's he called again?'

'The gardien,' said Charles. 'And I don't think much of him.'

'Why not?'

'He's not professional enough. I don't know where they found him from.'

'It's probably because Monsieur Fornier left so quickly,' said Mrs Lenoir. 'They had to get someone in quickly and had little choice.'

'Well, I think he's perfectly pleasant,' said Mrs Moore. 'Don't you, Lottie?' Lottie nodded. 'He's a little bit scruffy, I suppose, but he made us feel welcome.'

Salad niçoise was served next with anchovies, artichokes, tomatoes and olives. It was soaked in an oily dressing, and Lottie only just managed to clear her plate.

'And now the most important course!' announced Mrs Lenoir. 'The cheese! See how French I've become, Roberta? I absolutely adore cheese.'

'And quite right too, although I'm not sure I have space left for much.'

'Nonsense! There is always space for cheese. And I insist you try each one, Roberta.'

Lottie felt a little queasy as the silver cheese platters were laid on the table and the pungent odour drifted over to her. If she'd had nothing else to eat, she'd have been happy to eat the cheese. But the meal was becoming a struggle.

'We have Roquefort, Camembert and Époisses de Bourgogne,' said Mrs Lenoir.

'Époisses was a favourite of Napoleon's,' said Jacques. 'First made by Cistercian monks in the sixteenth century and after that—'

'Thank you, Jacques,' said Madeleine. 'But our visitors don't want to hear about the history of cheese.'

'It's not just any cheese,' he said. 'It's Époisses.'

'For once, I'm going to agree with Jacques,' said Charles. 'Époisses is my favourite cheese.' He handed a basket of bread to Lottie and she took the smallest slice.

'Where have the dogs got to?' asked Mrs Lenoir.

'They were under the table a short while ago,' said Lottie.

'Were they? Oh, how funny.' Mrs Lenoir leant over and peered beneath the table. 'I can only see Rosie there at the moment. Where's Edmond? Oh, he's a little rascal sometimes.'

A mountain of profiteroles was placed on the table for dessert.

'These all need to be eaten,' said Mrs Lenoir. 'They won't keep and I don't tolerate waste.'

'I'm sure the servants can finish them, Mother,' said Charles. 'I can only manage one.'

'One? How completely hopeless of you, Charles. You must have three, at the very least.'

Lottie loved cream and chocolate but, like Charles, she could barely face one profiterole now.

Eventually, the meal was over.

'I would suggest that we retire to the music room,' said Mrs Lenoir. 'But I want to find Edmond first. He'd better not have escaped onto a balcony again, he has so little sense that he'd jump off it.'

'Oh dear, that doesn't sound good,' said Mrs Moore, getting up from her seat.

'He's done it before,' said Mrs Lenoir. 'And it was pure luck that Pierre the delivery boy spotted him on the balcony and managed to catch him!'

'Pierre saved his life?' said Lottie.

'He did indeed.'

'Well, the chances are high that Pierre isn't loitering beneath a balcony this evening,' said Charles, propping himself up on his crutches. 'We'd better all go and look for that half-witted terrier.'

'There's no need to be rude about him, Charles!'

'I'm just pointing out that he's not too clever. I'm sure the corgi here wouldn't go leaping off a balcony.'

'Now I've got a terrible worry that Edmond's already jumped!' said Mrs Lenoir, heading for the door. 'Come on, everyone, get searching. I'll ask the servants to look too.'

'Oh, I hope he's not hurt!' said Madeleine, following her mother.

'Come on Rosie,' Lottie said to her dog. 'Can you lead me to your friend?'

Out in the corridor, Rosie trotted past the main staircase. Lottie followed and pushed open the first door she came to. She flicked on the light and saw the room was a study with a writing desk and shelves of books. A clock ticked loudly on the mantelpiece, the time was twenty minutes after nine. There was no sign of the black terrier. There was, however, a set of double doors which presumably led to a balcony. With the light on, it was difficult to see beyond them. So Lottie turned the light off and peered through the glass to the balcony outside. She tried one of the handles on the doors and opened it a little. She noticed how the iron bars of the balcony were spaced wide enough for a small dog to slip between them.

'There's no sign of Edmond here,' she said to Rosie. 'And don't you get any ideas about jumping off.'

The balcony overlooked a courtyard at the rear of the building. It was twilight now and the dark form of a tree loomed over a single lamppost and a bench. A blackbird trilled a melodic evening song and, in the lamplight's glow, Lottie saw a man. He wore a pale suit and a beret.

He glanced up at the building and Lottie stepped back out of view. She didn't want to be caught watching him. 'Come on, Rosie.' She ushered the dog back inside and closed the door.

The next room was a cosy sitting room. The light was on and Mrs Moore sat in a yellow chair by the fireplace.

'I had to have a sit down,' she said to Lottie. 'I've got a terrible stomach ache. I think it was the cheese. Or it could have been the fish. Or the duck. Perhaps the soup? I don't think it was the salad, but maybe it was the profiteroles? Oh dear, I've over-eaten!' Rosie sat by Mrs Moore's feet and she patted the dog on the head.

'I do hope Harriet isn't cross that I'm not searching for Edmond but, the truth is, I can't! She's over-fed me. I tell you what, though.' She lowered her voice and beckoned Lottie to come closer. 'If Harriet invites us to dinner again, we'll have to come up with an excuse. She's an excellent hostess, but isn't the conversation at the table difficult? Madeleine sulks, Charles barely says a word and that Jacques fellow... well, he's just dreadfully odd, isn't he? I found it quite an effort to make conversation at times. I have to hope I can arrange a series of social engagements with Prince Manfred and be able to excuse myself from any more of Harriet's dinner invitations. I don't mean to sound ungrateful, but I have to say what I feel, I'm afraid.'

'I understand you perfectly, Mrs Moore.'

'Thank you, Lottie. You're a sensible young woman.' She smiled. 'I'm pleased I employed you as my travelling companion. If I were doing this alone, then it would be quite unbearable at times!' She gave a chuckle. 'Anyway, I suppose I'd better get out of this comfortable chair and make an effort. Hopefully, there's not much of the evening left to get through. Oh, look who it is!'

Edmond the black terrier skipped through the door and greeted Rosie.

'We found him, Lottie! Didn't we do a good job?' She laughed. 'Let's go and tell them the news.'

Lottie, Mrs Moore and the two dogs made their way out to the corridor. They were just approaching the main staircase when they heard a shout from the floor above. First in French, then in English.

'Someone call the police! And a doctor!'

Chapter Seven

CHARLES APPEARED on the staircase and awkwardly descended on his crutches. His face was pale. 'It's Jacques!' he said. 'He's been attacked!'

Mrs Moore let out a shriek. 'Attacked? How?'

'There's been an intruder, things have been knocked about and drawers have been pulled out! They must have just left!'

Madeleine and her mother appeared on the stairs behind him.

'What's happened?' said Madeleine.

'It's Jacques, he's been attacked. He's on the floor of the sitting room!'

'What?' shrieked Madeleine. She dashed back up the stairs.

'I think he might be dead,' Charles said to his mother as they stood on the staircase. 'I tried rousing him, but there was no response.'

'*Dead*?'

'One of the lamps is on the floor next to him, I think the intruder hit him with it.'

'Can this really be happening?'

A maid appeared and Mrs Lenoir spoke to her in French, telling her to check that the police and a doctor had been summoned. Then she descended the stairs and spoke to Mrs Moore, trembling. 'I don't understand,' she said. 'How did they get in? Someone must have seen them!'

'They can't have got far,' said Mrs Moore.

'I'll go and see,' said Lottie, dashing in the direction of the front door.

'Be careful, Lottie!' Mrs Moore called after her.

Lottie reached the main entrance hall and saw the door was standing open. It was clear the culprit had left in a hurry. Lottie peered out into the stairwell, but all was silent. Then, with Rosie in tow, she descended the stairs to the lobby of the apartment block. There was nothing to see and the main door which opened out onto the street was shut.

Had the intruder come this way? Or perhaps they'd used another exit? She went over to the gardien's door and knocked.

'It's the English girl!' said Lucien Boucher with a smile. But the smile quickly faded from his face. 'What's happened?'

'Someone's been attacked! An intruder got in!'

The bell rang at the main door, and Lottie stepped aside to allow Mr Boucher to answer it.

Two police officers in round flat caps and capes rushed into the lobby. They asked directions to the Lenoir family's apartment before running up the staircase.

'Did you see anyone?' Lottie asked Lucien Boucher.

'No one. I didn't see a soul!'

LOTTIE AND ROSIE returned to the apartment where everyone now gathered in the sitting room with the yellow armchairs. Madeleine sat in one of the chairs sobbing while

Harriet Lenoir perched on the armrest and tried to console her.

Mrs Moore sat in the other chair, her face sombre. Charles paced across the room on his crutches. 'I can't believe it,' he said. 'I thought I'd check the drawing room and when I turned the light on, there he was! Sprawled face down on the floor by the sideboard. The lamp was on the floor next to him. He must have disturbed the intruder.'

'So the intruder was in there in the dark?' said Mrs Lenoir.

'He must have been. And I can only guess Jacques turned the light on and saw him there. The intruder panicked and attacked him.'

'But why didn't the intruder just run away?' said Madeleine, her face was red and wet. 'Why did he murder Jacques?'

'Perhaps he didn't intend to murder him,' said Charles. 'Perhaps he only intended to disable him. It's a heavy lamp base though. One blow from that to the back of the head could be... well, we know now... fatal.'

Madeleine began sobbing again.

'It's interesting that the murderer took the time to turn the light off when he left the room,' said Mrs Moore.

'And yet he didn't have time to close the main door behind him,' said Lottie. 'It was standing open when I went out.'

'Maybe the light was never on?' said Mrs Lenoir.

'Jacques must have turned it on,' said Charles. 'How else could he have looked in there for Edmond?'

'I don't understand why no one saw him,' said Mrs Moore. 'He got in and out of the apartment and none of us caught a glimpse of him!'

'I don't understand that either,' said Mrs Lenoir.

'I've just had a thought,' said Charles. 'Is Father's old revolver still stored in the drawing room?'

'Yes, it is,' said his mother.

'It's just as well the intruder didn't find it! Otherwise, he could have shot us all!'

'It's not loaded.'

'Where's the ammunition?'

'In a little box next to it.'

'So he could have shot us! If he knew something about loading and firing revolvers. Just think how much worse it could have been! You should keep things like that under lock and key, Mother.'

'You're right.'

A thick-set man in a dark suit appeared in the doorway, he puffed on a pipe before addressing them. 'Good evening everyone,' he said in French. 'I'm Commissaire Gauthier from the Brigade criminelle of the Police judiciaire. I have to speak with each of you about the events which have unfolded here this evening. Who found the body?'

'Me.' Charles raised his hand.

'Then I shall speak with you first.'

LOTTIE'S TURN with the commissaire came an hour later. They sat in the music room at a small cards table. A uniformed officer perched on a piano stool nearby.

'Do you know any French?' asked the commissaire.

'Yes.'

'Good. We'll speak in French then so my deputy can take notes. Name?'

'Lottie Sprigg.'

'Sprigg?'

'Yes.'

'Where are you from?'

'England.'

'Address in England?'

She gave him the address of Mrs Moore's home in Chelsea.

'Age?'

'Nineteen.'

'Occupation?'

'Travelling companion.'

'Travelling companion?' He puffed on his pipe.

'I'm an assistant to Mrs Moore. She employs me to accompany her on her travels.'

'How well did you know Jacques Marchand?'

'Not very well at all, I met him for the first time yesterday.'

'And what were your interactions with him?'

'Practically none.'

'You didn't speak to him?'

'I don't think I did, no.'

'Did you witness anything suspicious or unusual this evening?'

'No, nothing.'

'Where were you at half-past nine?'

'I was in the sitting room with my employer, Mrs Moore. We had just been looking for Edmond.'

'Edmond?'

'The dog.'

'Ah yes, I've heard about him.'

'And Edmond just walked into the room. We were pleased to finally find him and we were just going to tell the others when we heard that someone had been attacked.'

'Where were the others?'

'Upstairs I think.'

'Can you be more certain?'

'I don't know for certain, but Charles, Madeleine and Mrs Lenoir came down the stairs after the attack. I don't know where they were at the time of the attack.'

'So the only person you can provide an alibi for is Mrs Moore?'

'That's right.'

'Did you see anyone unusual in the apartment this evening?'

'I can't say that I'm familiar with all the staff here, but I didn't see anyone who looked out of place.'

'No one running away from the scene of the crime, for example?'

'No, no one.'

Lottie wondered if she should tell the commissaire that she'd seen Madeleine with another man. But she didn't want to incriminate Madeleine if the affair had nothing to do with Jacques's murder. For now, she kept quiet. She had to establish the facts first before repeating them to the police.

Chapter Eight

THE BANGING WAS SO loud that Tom Springer thought his door was about to give way.

'Give me a minute!' he shouted. He clambered out of bed and knocked over a glass with his foot. Stumbling over to the window, he opened the shutters a crack and winced as a shaft of bright sunlight hit him in the face.

The banging at the door resumed. 'Alright! I'm coming!' he called out.

Dazzled by the ray of sunshine, he groped around on the floor for his faded velvet robe and put it on. The floorboards were cold beneath his feet as he crossed the little apartment and unlocked the door.

'Tom!' Madeleine Lenoir fell into his arms.

'What is it, honey? What's happened?'

'It's Jacques! he's dead!'

'Dead? How?'

'He was murdered by an intruder!'

'*Murdered*? But that doesn't make sense, Jacques's not the sort to get murdered. Come inside.'

He closed the door, turned on the light and led Madeleine

over to a sunken sofa which had a stack of paintings leaning against it. She sat down, sobbing.

'Have a cigarette.' He offered her the packet he'd found in the pocket of his robe.

'I don't want one.'

He took a cigarette for himself, lit it, and inhaled deeply.

Jacques Marchand was dead. The wedding was off!

Tom couldn't deny he felt pleased about it, but the trouble was seeing Madeleine so upset.

'So what do you want, then? Coffee?'

Madeleine gave a sad nod.

Tom moved his easel so he could get into the poky kitchenette and put a pot of water to boil on the stove. The clock on the wall said half-past eight. It felt like the middle of the night, he rarely got up before midday.

The post from the previous day rested on the countertop. A letter and cheque from his parents in America and another letter which he had to hide. But where could he hide it? He glanced about the kitchenette. Behind the coffee pot? Beneath the stack of plates? Someone would easily find it. He didn't need to keep the letter, in fact it was probably best he got rid of it.

'Tom!' came Madeleine's voice from the sofa.

'Just doing the coffee, darling.'

Panicking, he grabbed the post, picked up his cigarette lighter and set light to the paper. He dropped it into the sink and watched it curl and blacken in the orange flame. Then he puffed on his cigarette to mask the burning smell with tobacco smoke.

He made the coffee and took it to Madeleine, who slumped across half the sofa.

'I must say you seem rather more upset about this than I thought you would, Maddy.'

'It's a shock. I've never known anyone get murdered before. It's all so sudden!'

'It certainly is.' He squashed his cigarette stub into the overflowing ashtray on the coffee table and sat down next to her. 'An intruder? You mean a burglar?'

'Yes. It was in the drawing room. They pulled out the drawers and took some silver, just small things. Mother's trying to work out what exactly. But Jacques disturbed them and now he's dead! Poor Jacques! Even though he was annoying and boring, I can't believe he's gone!'

'Surely you must feel a little bit relieved?' asked Tom.

'No, I don't! What a thing to say!'

'So you mean to tell me that all that moaning about having to marry him was just for show? Did you care about him, after all?'

'No, I didn't care about him. Well, I cared about him a little bit, but only because he was a friend. But I didn't love him!'

'Are you sure?'

'Yes, of course I'm sure! You know I didn't love him, Tom. I love you! But I can still be sad that he's dead!'

'I suppose so.'

'Aren't you sad?'

'Not particularly. I'm saddened because it's a tragedy, but for utterly selfish reasons, I'm rather pleased he's no longer around.'

'Poor Jacques! He was so innocent!'

'Was he?'

'Yes!'

'What about those stories of him being mean to Florence's cats?'

'That's just Florence, she likes to make a fuss.'

Madeleine was calmer now and Tom felt pleased she'd stopped sobbing, it had made her face all ugly and red.

Madeleine sipped her coffee. 'There's a girl who's seen us together,' she said.

'Who?'

'Lottie Sprigg, she's an assistant to one of Mother's friends, an American called Mrs Moore.'

'Sprigg? What sort of name is that?'

'She's from England. Maybe it's an English name. Anyway, I met her two days ago on a boring boat trip which Mother arranged and then she saw us together that evening when we were going to Jerome's. She passed us on the street.'

'Why didn't you point her out to me?'

'I didn't want to draw attention to it at the time and I wasn't sure if she recognised me. But at dinner last night, I noticed her looking at me.'

'Of course she's going to look at you, honey.'

'No, I mean in a suspicious way which suggests she saw us together.'

'Would she tell anyone do you think?'

'I don't know. Her employer Mrs Moore, I suppose. And then she might tell Mother.'

'And?'

'Well, Mother will know about us.'

'Just tell her I'm a friend.'

'She thinks I was with Chloe the other evening.'

'So you bumped into me on the street on the way to Chloe's? Isn't that right?'

'I suppose so.'

'Don't go worrying yourself over some English girl with a strange name.'

'Alright then. Can I have a cigarette now?'

'Sure.' He handed her the packet. It was almost empty, and he needed to buy another. He'd have to cash his parents' cheque before he did that. His parents' cheque... He jumped up and went into the kitchenette.

'Are you alright, Tom?'

'I'm doing just fine.' He stared into the sink where a few wet ashes remained. He'd washed the remains of the burned letter down the plughole.

Along with his parents' cheque.

A heavy sickening sensation weighed in his belly. He would have to telephone them and tell them it had got lost in the post. They would send another, but how long was that going to take? Weeks.

Tom gave a long exhale, then returned to the sofa.

'How's your painting coming along?' Madeleine pointed to the half-finished picture on the easel.

'Badly.'

'What is it?'

He felt his jaw clench. He hated having to explain his art. 'It's a bowl on a table.'

'Is it?'

'I know it's not obvious, but it's how I see it.'

'Your style has changed ever since you met that Pablo Picasso at Teddy's party.'

'I was painting like this before I bumped into him, honey. It's the style these days. It's a movement.'

'When we first met, you were painting pretty gardens and lakes.'

He lit another cigarette and puffed out a plume of smoke. 'Do you prefer the pretty gardens and lakes?'

'Only because I can tell what they are. Unlike...'

Tom tightened a fist. 'I told you it was going badly. I tell you what... I'll destroy it.'

He leapt up and yanked the painting off the easel. He flung the picture onto the floor and raised his foot, ready to stamp on it.

'No, Tom, don't! I do like it really, it's... you're experimenting, I understand. You must never destroy your work!'

'Lots of artists destroy their work!'

'But you shouldn't!' Madeleine got to her feet, took his arm and guided him back to the sofa.

'You don't understand how difficult it is,' he said, quivering with upset.

'No, I don't.'

'If only I could do an ordinary job like a bank clerk or something like that. And earn a regular wage! But the only thing I know how to do is paint.'

'I realise how difficult it is for you, Tom.'

'Well, I don't think you do. And something else has gone wrong.'

'Oh no, what?'

'The cheque from my parents appears to have been lost in the post. I was expecting it a few days ago, and it's not turned up. It was supposed to last me three months. I can ask them to send another, but in the meantime...'

'You need to borrow more money?'

He gave her a pleading look. 'I'm afraid so. I feel dreadful asking you again as you've been so generous already. When the cheque arrives, I'll be able to repay you. I know I already owe you a bit, I can settle all of it when they send the next cheque. But it will take a few weeks from America, you know what it's like.'

'It's fine.' She took his hand, and he gave her his widest smile.

'Thank you, honey.'

'It won't be much, I'm afraid. I don't know what's going to happen now.'

'What do you mean by that?' He felt the smile leave his face.

'Well, now that Jacques is dead.'

'What does he have to do with it?'

'Well, Mother was relying on his family's money, you see.

We don't have much left. In fact, everything Father left us has practically gone.'

'What?'

'Why do you look so worried, Tom? It doesn't matter. After all, it's only money.'

'So your family has nothing?'

'Well, I suppose we would if Mother sold some things. But why do you think she wanted me to marry Jacques in the first place?'

'She wanted you to marry well. She'd have never let you marry someone like me.'

'Well, there is that, status is important. But it was mainly about money.'

A chill ran over him. What had happened to the Lenoir family money? He'd assumed it would never run out.

'But it doesn't matter because you're going to be a famous artist, aren't you, Tom? And your paintings will sell for thousands of dollars one day. That's what you told me.'

'Yes, that's right, Maddy.' All he could do was pray it would come true. 'But it's a journey to get there.'

'Of course it is. And I'll be with you every step of the way.'

'Thank you, honey. I waited for you last night, by the way. I thought you'd stood me up.'

'Oh, of course, it was all that awful business with Jacques.' She clasped a hand to her mouth. 'I had forgotten about it for a moment and now it's all come back again. We were up most of the night speaking to the police. I wanted to come and see you, but I couldn't.'

'I get it.'

She rested her head against his shoulder. 'I don't know what I'd do without you.'

'That's kind of you to say, Maddy.'

'Oh, but it's not kind. It's how I feel! I do love you, you know that, don't you?'

'And I love you too, sweetie.' He kissed her hair.

'I should get back home now, the police are coming back today and Mother will need me there.'

'Well, you look after yourself now and try not to get too upset. It's sad news that Jacques is dead, but it's probably a good thing in the long run.'

'A good thing?' She sat up and stared at him, her eyes wide and damp.

'Did you want to spend the rest of your life married to him?'

'No.'

'Well, there you go.'

Chapter Nine

MRS MOORE PICKED over her croissant, then sat back in her chair and sipped her glass of orange juice. 'How awful to think there was a murdering intruder in that apartment, Lottie! We shall have to visit Harriet a little later and see how she's getting on. I can't imagine those children of hers being an enormous comfort to her. What she needs at the moment is the sympathy of a friend. And how awful for her that Madeleine will no longer be marrying into such a prestigious family! Harriet was clearly pinning a lot on that wedding and now she's lost it all! Who's Madeleine going to marry now?'

'The man I saw her walking with the other evening,' said Lottie. Then she stopped herself, realising what she'd said. She hadn't meant to tell Mrs Moore, and now her employer was staring at her, aghast.

'Another man? You must have been mistaken, Lottie, she was due to marry Jacques next month.'

Lottie cut off a piece of croissant and dropped it down to Rosie, who sat beneath the breakfast table. 'I probably was mistaken. Please don't say anything to Mrs Lenoir.'

'You're rarely mistaken though, are you, Lottie? Perhaps it was her? Oh dear, what a mess.'

'He could have just been a friend.'

'Let's hope he was. How did you come across them? What were you doing at the time?'

'I was walking back to the hotel after taking the message to Prince Manfred.'

'And he still hasn't replied, has he?'

'I'm sure he's very busy.'

'Yes, I'm sure he is.' She sighed and helped herself to a grape from a bowl of fruit. 'I can only hope Harriet finds another suitable man for Madeleine. She spent a lot of time arranging that marriage and it won't be easy to find another, especially with the shortage of men these days. It's difficult finding a good husband. You'll discover that, Lottie, when your turn comes.'

'I'm not in any hurry to find myself a husband.'

'You say that, but you might encounter a suitor on our travels. Who knows?'

Lottie felt too young to be thinking about a husband, she spread some butter onto a piece of croissant and hoped her employer would change the subject.

Mrs Moore rubbed at her brow. 'I knew it,' she said.

'What is it?'

'I've got another headache coming on. It always seems to happen after a murder, have you noticed that?'

BACK IN MRS MOORE'S hotel room, Lottie fetched the headache powders as her employer climbed into bed. 'It's such a shame I need a lie down. I'm supposed to be comforting Harriet later and yet I'm in no fit state for anything.'

After she'd taken her headache powders, Mrs Moore pulled a sleep mask over her eyes. 'Just leave me here, Lottie. I need to remain still and quiet while the medicine does its work.'

Lottie was about to go to her neighbouring room when there was a knock at the door.

'Oh no,' whimpered Mrs Moore. 'We should have put a notice on the door requesting to be left in peace.'

A messenger boy gave Lottie an envelope, it was addressed to Mrs Moore in a flamboyant hand.

'It's for you,' she said to her employer.

'Well, it can probably wait, then. Or maybe it's from poor Harriet, in which case we'd better read it now. Can you open it and read it to me, please, Lottie?'

Lottie did so. It was an invitation written out on stiff card with a gilded gold edge.

'"His Royal Highness Manfred Ludwig Franz Wilhelm Prinz von Bayern cordially invites you to the Vernissage de L'Exposition des Beaux-Arts at the Grand Palais des Champs-Élysées, Paris."'

'What?' Mrs Moore sprang into a sitting position, her face mask still over her eyes. 'What was that? I've no idea what it means, but it sounds wonderful! When?'

'This evening.'

LOTTIE AND ROSIE took Mrs Moore's immediate reply to the Ritz Hotel. Then Lottie decided to take Rosie for a stroll in the Jardin des Tuileries nearby. They passed the bakery and came across Pierre loading fresh bread into the basket on the front of his bicycle. He paused from his work as soon as he noticed Lottie and beckoned her over. Even though she'd just eaten breakfast, the aroma of fresh bread made her mouth water.

'You were there at the dinner party, weren't you?' He kept

his voice low. 'I took your message to Mrs Lenoir to say you'd attend. Did you see the murderer?'

'No. If only I had!'

'How did no one see him?'

'I don't know! There's been no sighting at all. Have there been any similar burglaries or attacks around here recently?'

'I don't think so. I know one of the maids who works for the Lenoirs and she didn't see anything either. Maybe he was hiding in the building?'

'Where?'

'I don't know.'

'Is there a way into the building which the intruder could have used without being seen?' asked Lottie.

'There's a door at the back.'

'So he could have got in and out that way?'

'I think it's usually locked. The gardien makes sure of that.'

'It's a mystery.'

'It could be that American man I've seen Madeleine Lenoir with.'

'You've seen her with him, too? He wears a beret?'

'Yes. He tries to look French, but he doesn't speak a word of it.'

'Who is he?'

'An artist, I've heard. He probably didn't want her to marry Monsieur Marchand, so he murdered him.'

'That reminds me!' said Lottie.

'Of what?' Pierre's eyes brightened.

'Yesterday evening I saw a man wearing a beret in the courtyard at the back of the building!'

'There you go!'

'Do you think it was him?'

'It must have been!'

Lottie felt her heart pound. Should she tell the police this information?

'Pierre!' The baker appeared in the doorway. 'Stop talking to girls and get on with your deliveries before that bread goes stale!'

Chapter Ten

'How are you this morning, Madame Lenoir?' asked Commissaire Gauthier. He made himself comfortable in a yellow armchair in the sitting room.

'I've been better,' said Harriet. She noticed how tightly her hands were clasped in her lap. She was nervous, even though she shouldn't be. This was her home, and the detective was here to help her. Everything would hopefully be resolved satisfactorily. Edmond sat by her feet, she gave him a little pat on the head and it helped her feel slightly better.

'I have a few more questions for you today,' said the detective. 'I hope you don't mind?'

'No.' She did mind, but there was no use in saying so.

'Do you mind if I smoke my pipe?'

'No.' She minded this too, but she didn't want to get on the wrong side of the detective.

'Have you discovered exactly what was taken in the robbery last night?' he asked.

'Yes, not much. Just some silver from some of the drawers.'

'What sort of silver?'

'A tobacco box, a cigarette case, a little jewellery box, some napkin rings, a hip flask... they don't sound like much, but some of them belonged to my late husband.'

'I'm sorry to hear it.'

Harriet pulled a handkerchief from the sleeve of her dress and dabbed her eyes. 'The thief must have been emptying the drawers when Monsieur Marchand disturbed him.'

'Very likely.'

'They didn't need to kill him, though!'

'Perhaps the intention wasn't to kill, Madame Lenoir? Maybe they just wished to stun him so they could make a getaway. The post-mortem examination of the victim might tell us how many times he was hit. But it's possible only one strike was all that was needed. It was a heavy lamp base. Marble I believe.'

'Green onyx.'

'Thank you for the correction.'

Harriet felt a sob rise from her chest. 'It's awful, Jacques was due to marry my daughter next month!'

'It is awful indeed.' He puffed on his pipe. 'How many members of staff do you employ here, Madame Lenoir?'

'Eight.'

'And you had how many guests to dinner? Five?'

'That's correct.'

'So, including yourself, there were six people eating dinner and eight members of staff in the apartment. Fourteen people in the apartment in total. And no one saw anything?'

'No. I don't understand it.'

'And what were you doing at the time of the attack?'

'You asked me that question yesterday evening, Commissaire.'

'I hope you don't mind me asking again, sometimes it is necessary.'

She realised he was repeating his question because he wanted to check she gave the same answer. So he suspected her after all! He wasn't here to help, he was here to catch her out!

She fixed his gaze, and he stared back at her, unblinking. 'I was in one of the bedrooms on the upstairs floor when I heard Charles raise the alarm.'

'That was when he raised the alarm, how about just before then?'

'I was in one of the bedrooms.'

'Which one?'

'A guest bedroom. It overlooks the street at the front. We call it the blue bedroom because the furnishings are, well, they're blue. I was looking for my dog Edmond in there. He likes to sleep on the beds even though he's not allowed to. I was in that room while the intruder attacked Monsieur Marchand.'

'Did anyone see you in there?'

'No! We were all in different places looking for Edmond.'

The commissaire made some notes. 'It's very interesting indeed. I would have expected some witnesses to have come forward by now.'

'What do you mean by that?'

'We're here in the middle of Paris, it's a busy place! There are two other households in this building and they both employ staff. Twenty-three people in total.'

'That many?'

'Including your household that makes thirty-seven, and the gardien makes it thirty-eight. Out on the street are cafes and restaurants which were open at the time of the attack, and they all had customers. I'm surprised we haven't yet found anybody either in this building or out on the street who saw someone suspicious entering or leaving the building. The culprit would have been desperate to get away, don't you think? He must have been in a hurry.'

'Yes. He left our door wide open!'

'Yet no one saw him.'

'So what are you suggesting, Commissaire?'

'I think I need to consider the people who were in the building.'

'No!'

'We can't rule anything out.'

'Nobody in this household would ever dare do such a thing! My staff are extremely loyal and hard-working.'

'It's not unheard of for servants to steal from their employers.'

'I realise that. But none of my staff have ever stolen from me!'

'Let's imagine for a moment, it was a member of your staff, Madame Lenoir. He or she could have been so horrified that Monsieur Marchand caught them in the act of stealing from you, that they knocked him to the ground and made their escape.'

'I suppose it's a possibility. But extremely unlikely.'

'I don't think the culprit entered that room intending to commit murder,' said the commissaire. 'Everything suggests Monsieur Marchand disturbed him or her and they reacted.'

'It won't have been a member of my staff, Commissaire. And besides, the main door was left open!'

'We shouldn't ignore the possibility that the culprit opened the door in order to make it look like the assailant had fled. It could have been done to fool us.'

'How would someone even think of that?'

'You'd be surprised.' He puffed out a ring of tobacco smoke. 'Can you tell me a little more about your family, Madame Lenoir?'

She felt a snap of irritation. 'What do they have to do with anything?'

'It helps me to have a better understanding of you all.'

'Does it?' She sighed and told him all about the wedding which had been planned.

'How did your daughter feel about the marriage?'

Harriet caught her breath. She had to make sure the commissaire believed every word she told him. 'She was excited about it. She loved him dearly and couldn't wait to be his wife...' she allowed a sob to interrupt her. 'I can't believe the wedding isn't taking place now! Madeleine is devastated. We all are!'

The detective gave an understanding nod. 'And what was the relationship between your son and Monsieur Marchand like?'

'I hope you're not accusing my son of murder!'

'Absolutely not, Madame Lenoir. This is all for my own personal understanding.'

'They got on very well. They are - were - quite different to each other, but that's the reason they got on.'

'Was there any altercation or misunderstanding between either of your children and Monsieur Marchand?'

'No! None.'

'One of my men has told me that your son is engaged to a young lady called Florence Vidal.'

'Yes he is.'

'And she was previously engaged to Monsieur Marchand.'

'How on earth did he find that out?'

'It's what we do at the Brigade criminelle, Madame Lenoir. We're detectives.'

Harriet felt her hands tremble a little.

'So is that right?' he asked.

'Is what right?'

'That Monsieur Marchand was previously engaged to your son's fiancée?'

'Yes, it's right. But there was no ill-feeling between them about it. Everyone got on extremely well.'

'I'm pleased to hear it, Madame Lenoir.'

She didn't like the faint smile which played on his lips.

Chapter Eleven

Lottie breathed in the blossom-scented air in the Jardin des Tuileries. Two small children raced past her on the long path and a lady pushing a large-wheeled perambulator followed them. Rosie sniffed at the colourful blooms in a tidy flowerbed.

Lottie was busy puzzling out how someone could have got in and out of the Lenoir's apartment building. Had they used the door at the rear which Pierre said was usually locked? And could the intruder have been Madeleine Lenoir's American artist friend? She'd seen a man resembling him in the court-yard shortly before the murder. Surely the rear door was accessible from the courtyard? She wondered if she could have a look at the location herself.

'Miss Sprigg?'

Lottie had been so distracted by her thoughts that she hadn't noticed Madeleine Lenoir approach.

The young woman wore a sombre grey overcoat, her face was pale and her eyes looked red and tired.

'Miss Lenoir! I'm so sorry about what happened to Jacques, it must be—'

She gave a dismissive wave. 'Thank you, there's no need to say too much about it. And call me Maddy.'

'Alright.'

'I thought I'd come here for a walk and calm my mind. I brought my book with me too.' It was in her hand. 'I thought I might sit on a bench and read some detective stories.'

'I like detective stories too.'

'Do you?' Madeleine smiled.

'It's a lovely morning to be sitting on a bench and reading,' said Lottie. The sun shone and birdsong carried from the trees.

Rosie trotted over to Madeleine and sniffed her leg. The young woman smiled and patted the corgi on the head. Lottie assumed Madeleine would then continue her walk, but she remained where she was. 'I'm so sorry that tragedy struck when you were our guests for dinner,' she said.

'Thank you, but it's not your fault.'

'I know. But it's unpleasant for you, you probably think this sort of thing happens in Paris all the time.'

'No, not at all. It's a terrible tragedy and hopefully the police will discover who's behind it.'

Madeleine scratched her nose. 'There's something I need to speak to you about, Miss Sprigg.'

'Lottie.'

'Alright then, Lottie.' She smiled. 'I know you saw me the other evening.'

'Well, I wasn't completely sure it was you because you looked different.'

'I was dressed up for the evening. Jacques didn't like to go out to parties, he said they bored him. And he didn't like to dance either! But I love to do those things, so I have some other friends to socialise with. Jacques knew some of them, but not all of them - they weren't really his sort of people. I'm someone who's always liked to have a lot of friends and there were times when I liked to go out with them and have fun. I'm not saying I did anything behind his back, if he ever asked me then I would happily tell him everything. I'm not the sort to keep secrets. I'm just trying to explain why you saw me the other evening and why I was with a friend. I realise how it might look and how some people might get the wrong idea. Tom - that's who you saw me with - is just a good friend of mine. I didn't tell Jacques about him because I knew Jacques wouldn't like him. But if he'd asked me then I'd have told him about him. And really, there wasn't much to tell. I'm sure you understand, Lottie.'

'I do.'

'Good.' Madeleine gave a relieved smile. 'We're a similar age, aren't we? I'm sure many girls our age would do the same. We don't want to grow old too quickly, do we? Where are you heading?'

'I'm going to take Rosie up to the pond, round it and back again.'

'The Grand Basin Rond. I'll come with you.' Madeleine now took Lottie's arm, as if they were good friends. 'What I'd really like to say is that I'd be extremely grateful if you were to not mention that you saw Tom and I together the other evening. I know it sounds an odd request, and you really must understand that I have nothing to hide. But I think, at the moment, it might just complicate things a little. I think if the police were to find out, they would start questioning me about my feelings towards Jacques. And to be quite honest with you, Lottie, my feelings towards him were complicated. I loved him, of course I did, and I was very much looking forward to being his wife. But we were quite different, and I always knew I wanted the sort of marriage where we could follow our own pursuits occasionally and not live in each other's pockets. It was something I was going to discuss with him before our wedding day.' Her voice choked. 'But before I could, someone killed him!'

A small black cat skipped across the path. Rosie set off after it, barking.

'Rosie!' Lottie dashed after her and eventually the dog came scampering back.

'I'm sorry, Maddy,' said Lottie, as she clipped the lead to Rosie's collar. 'My dog interrupted you.'

'Oh, it's alright.' Madeleine gave a sigh. 'I think what I'm trying to say is there are lots of things Jacques and I needed to discuss before we got married. Our relationship wasn't perfect, but I had ideas on how to set that right before our wedding day. And now I won't ever get the chance! It's going to look to the police as if I was treating him cruelly.'

'Why would they think that?'

'Because of my other friendships. Friendships with people like Tom, for example. And if people find out about him, then they're going to assume we were having a love affair. And it's simply not true. You believe me though, don't you, Lottie?' She tightened her grip on Lottie's arm.

'Yes.' Lottie knew she couldn't say much else.

'So we're agreed then?'

'On what?'

'About you seeing me and Tom. There's no need to mention it to anyone at all. Not for now anyway, perhaps after the police have caught the killer, then it would be fine to say it. But at the moment, everyone's going to be grasping at whatever information they can.'

'But surely it was a burglar who carried out the attack?' Lottie wasn't sure if she believed this now, but she decided to put it to Madeleine.

'Oh yes, of course it was. The trouble is, no one has seen the burglar and the longer the police can't find him, the more they're going to look at other possible suspects. I worry people assume Tom and I were having a love affair, and that I didn't care about Jacques. At the very worst, they might think I wanted Jacques out of the way! And that's such an awful thought!' Her voice broke into a sob and she stopped to wipe her eyes with a handkerchief.

Lottie felt the need to console her new friend by putting a hand on her shoulder and saying some comforting words. But it was difficult to be certain that Madeleine was telling her the truth.

Chapter Twelve

CHARLES LENOIR SAT in the study, listening to the steady tick of the clock on the mantelpiece. The detective had been talking to his mother for nearly an hour. Why was it taking so long?

He suspected it was his turn next, even though he'd already had a lengthy conversation with the police the previous evening. It was obvious they suspected him because he was the one who'd found Jacques Marchand's body. He'd never liked the man, and that counted against him, too. He had to convince them he was innocent, but it was difficult to know how.

Jacques's death changed everything. The wedding which everyone had been talking about for the past six months would no longer happen. What were they going to do for money now? His salary as a trainee solicitor wasn't a lot but it was enough to support him and his future wife, Florence. But what about his mother and sister?

'Oh, you're in here.' Madeleine appeared in the doorway looking every inch the grieving fiancée. She wore a drab, grey dress and a weary, tired expression. He wondered how upset she really was. 'What are you doing?' she asked.

'What does it look like I'm doing?'

'I don't know. Sitting about.'

'Exactly. I'm waiting for the detective to finish talking to Mother. Where've you been?'

'I had to go out for a walk.'

'*Had* to?'

'Yes, my mind has been spinning around and around.' She sauntered over to a bookcase, put a book in it and pulled out another. 'It's just dreadful Charles. I don't know what to think.'

He could feel his patience with his sister fading already. 'It's easy to know what to think. A robber entered the house, Jacques caught him, then the robber whacked him over the head with a lamp base.'

'Oh, how could you put it so bluntly?' Madeleine's face crumpled, and she sank into a chair by the bookcase.

'Don't pretend you cared about him that much,' said Charles. 'I know you didn't want to marry him.'

'How dare you! I did care about him! What are you suggesting? That I murdered him because I didn't want to marry him and made it look like a robbery?'

'I wasn't saying that, but now you've suggested it—'

'Oh Charles, you can be so hateful!' She hurled the book at him and he caught it before it hit him in the chest. 'What a thing to say!'

'I didn't say anything! You were the one who suggested a motive.'

'And you were the one who found him! I think you killed him because he was supposedly mean to Florence and her cats.'

He stifled a laugh. 'You think I'd risk the guillotine for Florence and her pets?'

'Possibly. And I don't think he was mean to them, it's just something Florence said. He told me he couldn't step through her front door without sneezing a dozen times. He asked her politely to get them out of the way whenever he visited and she took it badly. It wouldn't surprise me if she told you to get rid of him as revenge.'

He gave a snort. 'Ridiculous!'

'I expect she's happy he's dead.'

'I shouldn't think she's happy at all! I don't know how she feels about it yet, I haven't seen her since it happened. But I sent her a telegram late last night and I'm going to call on her later.'

'She'll be over the moon, I'm sure of it.'

It was difficult to believe his sister was twenty years old, she could be so childish. He took a breath and attempted to calm the conversation. 'Nobody is over the moon about Jacques's death, Maddy. No matter what some of us thought about him, his murder is a tragedy. I don't honestly believe you had anything to do with it, it's quite obvious that he disturbed an intruder. He was in the wrong place at the wrong time and we have to hope the police catch the thief before he does the same to someone else.'

'You do realise that you and I could become suspects if the police don't catch the thief?'

'Yes, which is why I want him found as soon as possible! Meanwhile, the detective is wasting his time interviewing Mother for hours. They have all the information they need, they have to be out there looking for him now. Someone will have seen him.'

'Perhaps one of the servants did it?'

'Which one?'

'I don't know. But it explains why no one saw the intruder.'

'The police have spoken to all the servants and I'm sure

they'll speak to them again. If it is one of them, then the police will work it out soon enough. I don't believe it's one of them, though. Why choose a time when we're all wandering about the house looking for the dog? If I were a servant wishing to steal from my employer, then I'd creep into the room in the middle of the night when no one else was about. Or I'd do it gradually. Sneaking into the room and taking something here and there over the course of a few weeks. The intruder had pulled out drawers and thrown them about. That suggests he was in a hurry to get what he could while he had a chance.'

'Perhaps it was that American lady or her assistant.'

Charles laughed. 'And why would they steal from us?'

'I don't know. We don't know them, do we? Mrs Moore is an old friend of Mother's, but we don't know much about her.'

'We know she's rich and doesn't need to steal from people.'

'Well, we don't know that Lottie girl at all. Maybe she's prone to thieving?'

'And murdering? She doesn't seem the type.'

'No one seems the type though, do they? That's how they get away with it.'

'I think you're talking nonsense, Maddy. As usual.'

Her face crumpled again. 'How can you say such a thing to me when my fiancé has just been murdered?'

Charles sighed, certain her tears weren't genuine. 'This is just typical of Jacques.'

'What do you mean?'

'Well, out of all of us in this apartment building, it had to be him, didn't it? He was the one who ended up being the victim. He was just that sort of person.'

'Are you saying it's his fault?'

'Not directly. But Jacques was the sort of man who had the uncanny ability to bring things onto himself.'

Chapter Thirteen

LOTTIE PASSED a newsstand as she returned to the hotel and noticed Jacques Marchand's murder in the headlines. She bought a newspaper and showed it to Mrs Moore once she was in her room.

'I can't read it, it's in French.' She sat at her dressing table and Lottie could see she'd been writing letters. No doubt she was telling her friends about the grim event the previous evening.

'I'll translate it then,' said Lottie, taking a seat on a little upholstered stool by the window. 'It won't be perfect, though.'

'No need for perfection, Lottie. Just the general gist is fine.'

'"Jacques Marchand, forty-five—"'

'Forty-five?'

'Sorry, I meant twenty-five. "The son of... something... politician, Louis Marchand, who is... something... mayor of the 16th arrondissement in July."'

'What do you mean by "something"?'

'That's for the bits I don't understand.'

'Oh, I see. So the article presumably describes how Louis Marchand is standing for election for mayor of the 16th arrondissement in July.'

'Yes, that must be it. "Monsieur Marchand was a student of mathematics at the University of Paris—"'

'And didn't we know it? He was talking about some theory or other, wasn't he? It went completely over my head.'

'And mine. "And he was engaged to be married to Madeleine Lenoir, daughter of the late politician Antoine Lenoir." Something, something.'

'Harriet doesn't get a mention, then?'

'I can't see her name here. "Monsieur Marchand was murdered by an intruder who broke into the Lenoir apartment on Rue Rouget de Lisle at half-past nine yesterday evening... something... the police are appealing to anyone who saw anything suspicious in the area at the time to contact them."'

'Well, that doesn't tell us anything we don't already know, does it? I think we should call on Harriet this afternoon and see how she's faring. How awful to have someone murdered in your own home! And all those wedding plans gone to waste. She was so looking forward to the wedding, wasn't she?'

'I bumped into Madeleine Lenoir in the Jardin des Tuileries.'

Mrs Moore's mouth gaped. 'She was out and about, was she? How unusual for someone whose fiancé has just been murdered. How was she?'

'Much as you would expect. She told me the man I saw her with was just a friend.'

'I hope he is, for her sake.'

'She doesn't want anyone to know about him in case they jump to the wrong conclusion.'

Mrs Moore shook her head. 'The poor child, she really has made a mess for herself hasn't she?'

. . .

AT LUNCHTIME, Mrs Moore showed Prince Manfred's invitation to the waiter.

'I feel very honoured to receive this,' she said. 'I realise it's an invitation of some sort, but I don't know what for. My assistant here has translated what she can, but neither of us knows what a vernissage is. Can you help?'

The waiter examined the invitation. 'It's a preview of an art exhibition. You're very lucky to be invited to it, it is a prestigious event.'

'I thought as much.'

'The gentleman who has invited you looks very important.'

'He is,' said Mrs Moore with a proud smile. 'I didn't realise he had quite so many names, either.' She thanked the waiter, and he went on his way. '"His Royal Highness Manfred Ludwig Franz Wilhelm Prinz von Bayern",' she recited from the invitation. 'Isn't that quite something, Lottie?' Her eyes glazed over a little, as if she were imagining married life with him in a Bavarian hill-top castle.

AFTER LUNCH, Lottie, Mrs Moore and Rosie made the short walk to the Lenoir apartment.

Stooped, scruffy Mr Boucher, answered the door. He didn't seem as cheery as he had the previous day.

'Hello again, my American friend, English friend and Italian dog. You're here to visit Madame Lenoir?' He shook his head. 'Such a terrible tragedy.'

'Did you see anything?' asked Mrs Moore.

'Me? No, nothing at all. The first I knew about it was when this young lady knocked on my door.' He gestured at Lottie. 'I feel like I've failed the Lenoir family.'

'Nonsense, of course you haven't failed them!'

'I have. I'm supposed to keep an eye on all the visitors. And to think I didn't spot an intruder!'

'He must have broken in somewhere.'

'But where? The door at the back was locked and there are no other windows or doors which have been broken or forced open.'

'Really? Well, that is strange.'

'I don't understand it at all. I admit the guests personally and I unlock the doors for them when they leave and I put all the details down in my little book. I haven't been here long, but I know all the residents and staff by sight. I make a note of everybody who comes and goes and somehow a man got into the building and committed that awful murder. I didn't even see him running away!'

'You really mustn't blame yourself, Mr Boucher,' said Mrs Moore. 'You did all you could.'

'But it wasn't enough!'

'Who else lives in this apartment building?' asked Lottie. 'Maybe they saw something?'

'You have the Chenault family on the second floor and the Picard family on the very top floor. I don't think anybody saw or heard anything. It's a mystery. That poor Jacques Marchand.'

'Did you know him?' asked Mrs Moore.

'I only spoke to him a couple of times, but he was a respectful and polite young man. He was quite pleasant for someone who comes from a wealthy family. Usually wealthy people are so rude! Well, they are to people like me, that's why I'm often rude in return!' He grinned. 'But on a more sombre note, I obviously feel very sad for the young man and his family and the Lenoir family, too. I've extended my condolences to Mrs Lenoir, but I don't think she likes me very much.'

'Really?'

'I think she preferred the previous man, Monsieur Fornier. But anyway, she has to put up with me now. Perhaps she'll like me one day. The important thing is that the police catch the man who did this awful murder. We can't sleep comfortably in our beds until he's caught!'

HARRIET LENOIR RECEIVED them in the sitting room with the yellow armchairs. She wore a black dress and looked weary. 'How nice to see your friendly face, Roberta, after that grumpy detective I had to speak to this morning.' Her black terrier, Edmond, greeted Rosie, and the two dogs skipped about together, oblivious to the mood.

'Has the detective made any progress?' asked Mrs Moore, settling into a chair.

'None! I think he'd much rather sit about puffing on his pipe and drinking my coffee than try to find the culprit.'

'Terrible.'

'Just awful. He's been interviewing me and my children as if we're all somehow to blame! There's no reason at all we would have wished to harm Jacques. In fact, I saw him as a saviour, for want of a better word. I have to be honest with you, Roberta. We've experienced a few financial difficulties recently.'

'No!'

'I'm afraid it's true. The money Antoine left us... well, we appear to have spent it! Charles is alright with his salary, but Maddy's marriage to Jacques would have secured her some much-needed income. That's not the sole reason she was engaged to marry him, of course. Then the awful events of yesterday evening put an end to it all! I don't know what to do now.'

'Perhaps I can lend you a little?'

'No Roberta, I won't hear of it. I have no wish to be a charity case. The answer is quite simple, I shall have to sell some of my belongings.'

'But what a shame! You have such a beautiful home.'

'I know. But it's the only sensible thing which can be done. In fact, I'm quite grateful that the intruder chose one of my cheaper lamps to attack Jacques with. At least the pair of Victorian marble lamps are unscathed and their sale alone will sustain us for a few months.'

'Selling all your lovely things can't be the answer, Harriet, at least let me help.'

'The need will only be temporary. In due course, Madeleine will find herself another husband. I know it sounds disrespectful of me to say so when her fiancé has just died, but it is reality. She is only twenty after all, and she'll meet another young wealthy man before long. And perhaps I could even consider marriage myself? Since Antoine's death, I haven't wished to give it any thought at all, but I'm realising that perhaps I can marry again. You set a good example, Roberta. By searching for your fourth husband, you've demonstrated that an unattached lady need not sit about and mope. In fact, this Bavarian prince you have your eye on sounds quite ideal.'

Mrs Moore's eyes narrowed. 'Ideal for my purposes, yes. He's not the sort of man who would appeal to you, Harriet.'

'Would he not? I've always liked the idea of marrying into royalty.'

'There are plenty of royal houses in Europe, I'm sure there will be someone among them who interests you. As for Prince Manfred, he's invited me to a preview of an art exhibition this evening at the Grand Palais des Champs-Élysées.'

'Has he indeed? Goodness, Roberta! You've clearly made an impression on him.'

'I think I must have.'

Chapter Fourteen

THAT EVENING, Mrs Moore, Lottie and Rosie were chauffeured in a shiny black motor car through the cobbled expanse of Place de la Concorde and onto the Champs-Élysées. An orange streak of sunset spread across the skyline.

It was only a short journey, but Mrs Moore would have struggled to walk far in her crimson gown. Lottie had never seen so much fabric in a dress before, it occupied most of the seat in the back of the car. She hoped, for Mrs Moore's sake, that Prince Manfred would be impressed. Lottie wore her new turquoise dress and felt proud to finally own an outfit which was vaguely fashionable.

'Is that the Arc de Triomphe up ahead?' asked Mrs Moore. 'Oh please ask the driver to take us to it, Lottie, I want to see it!'

Lottie asked the driver and he continued on to where the boulevard ended at the grand stone arch. 'Isn't it marvellous?' said Mrs Moore as the car circled the monument on a wide cobbled road. There were people standing beneath the arch, admiring it close up, and Lottie imagined they had to dodge the traffic to get there safely.

After its circuit, the car rejoined the Champs-Élysées and stopped a few moments later outside the opulent Grand Palais. It was decorated with columns and statues and had a large glass roof. It took the efforts of both Lottie and the chauffeur to get Mrs Moore and her enormous gown out of the car.

'What a wonderful place,' she said, admiring the building. 'Prince Manfred would never choose anywhere understated, would he?'

Lottie was amazed at the size of the place once they were inside. The wrought-iron roof arched high over their heads and the setting sun cast deep orange beams through the glass. But what amazed Lottie more was the vast number of people. Everyone was dressed in their finery and admiring the pictures and sculptures on display. Mrs Moore examined the scene through her lorgnette, which hung around her neck on a gold chain. 'I thought a preview would only be open to a select few,' she said. 'I wasn't expecting half of Paris to be here. We must be in a separate room somewhere with the prince. Please can you find out for me, Lottie?'

Lottie looked about and found a waiter with a silver tray of champagne filled glasses. 'Please can you tell me where we meet Prince Manfred?'

'I believe he is present.'

'We're wondering if there's a separate room somewhere. He invited us as his guests.'

'Everybody here is his guest this evening.' The waiter gestured at the crowd.

'Oh. Alright then. Thank you.'

Mrs Moore's shoulders slumped when Lottie relayed this information to her. 'Everyone here is Prince Manfred's guest?'

'Apparently so.'

'But I was expecting something a little more intimate, Lottie. Weren't you?'

'I suppose he has a lot of guests.'

'He does indeed. Well, maybe we should look at some of the art while we're here.'

Lottie accompanied Mrs Moore as she did a cursory turn around the room, glancing at the various artworks in their heavy gold frames. Her wide red dress cleared a pathway for her through the crowd.

'Well, that's all the art previewed,' said Mrs Moore, once they'd completed the round. 'So where's.... Oh!' She swiftly picked up her lorgnette. 'There he is!'

Lottie followed her gaze to a tall, plump man in a blue velvet frock coat. He was about fifty years old and had a head of fine curls, which were suspiciously thick and dark. He had a wide moustache with thin, waxed ends and a pink silk cravat was tied into a bow at his neck.

Mrs Moore dashed over to him while Lottie and Rosie stood in the centre of the crowd.

Lottie looked down at her dog. 'What do we do now? Maybe we can look at the paintings again?'

'Hello,' said a voice at her shoulder. The accent sounded American.

Lottie turned to see a young man in a crumpled, light linen suit. He wore a beret at a jaunty angle and held a thin cigarette between his fingers.

'I recognise you,' he said. 'But you don't know who I am, do you?'

'You're Tom.'

'Oh, you do know who I am?'

'I saw you with Madeleine Lenoir the other evening, and then she told me all about you when I bumped into her in the gardens this morning.'

'She did? Oh. I hope she didn't say too much.'

'She told me you're friends.'

He smiled. 'That's right, we are. And I remember seeing

you the other evening. You're Lottie, aren't you? I hope you haven't misunderstood the nature of my and Maddy's friendship.'

'No, not at all.'

'Good. So what brings you here?'

'I'm accompanying my employer, Mrs Moore. She was invited as a guest of Prince Manfred.'

'Was she indeed? I heard he arranged this party or whatever you call it.' He glanced about. 'It's not much of a party, is it? Anyway, I'm here because I'm an artist.'

'Is your work on display this evening?'

'Not this evening, no.' He gave an awkward grin. Lottie decided he would be quite handsome if he didn't have a wide, frog-like mouth. And she didn't like his manner of looking her up and down, she supposed it was something he did with all young women. 'One day, my work will be exhibited,' he said. 'The thing is, my art is more modern than a lot of the stuff they've got up on the walls in here. It's quite traditional, as you've probably noticed. I would say old-fashioned, but that's a little unfair. Let's just say that it doesn't challenge any rules.'

'But your work does?'

'Oh yes.' He inhaled on his cigarette. 'It's certainly avant-garde. I met Pablo Picasso at a party the other week.'

'I've heard of him.'

'He's Spanish, but lives in Paris these days. All the talented artists live here. I've been here for two years. I'm from New Hampshire and I had to get away, I couldn't handle prohibition. Have you noticed how many Americans there are in Paris right now?'

'Not really.'

'Well, there are loads. And we've all come here so we can buy a decent drink in a bar.'

'A long way to travel for a drink.'

He laughed. 'Well, it's not just for that reason alone. Paris is beautiful, don't you think?'

'Yes it is.'

'I wouldn't want to live anywhere else. You can be anyone you like here. My parents wanted me to go into banking like my father, but I always knew that I wanted to paint. In the little town where I grew up, you don't get people who paint for a living. I had to follow my heart and my passion.'

'Have you brought Maddy with you this evening?'

'No. It wouldn't be appropriate for her, she's in mourning having just lost her fiancé. She's taken it badly and understandably so. To think they were going to get married next month! And now it's all over.' He shook his head. 'Poor Maddy. You do understand we're just friends?'

'Yes.'

'Good. Anyway, the whole thing has been very frightening for Maddy and her family. That intruder could have attacked any one of them! I know it sounds awful to say it, but speaking from a selfish point of view, I'm quite relieved that it wasn't Maddy or her mother or brother who were attacked. It's awful about Jacques, but I didn't know him. It's difficult to mourn someone you don't know, isn't it?'

'I think I saw you last night.'

'Me?' A nervous smile played on his lips.

'I saw someone who looked like you in the courtyard behind the Lenoir family's apartment.'

'No, that wouldn't have been me.'

'He was wearing a beret just like yours.'

'Lots of people wear these berets.'

'And a similar suit. In fact, he was a similar build too.'

He took his cigarette from his lips and leaned into her. 'The fact of the matter, Lottie, is that I'm just an average looking fellow. There's nothing remarkable or immediately recognisable about me at all. So what if I wear a beret? I'm not the only one.'

There was a sneer on his wide lips, as if he'd tasted something unpleasant. Lottie decided not to argue with him, he was clearly keen to cover his tracks. But what was he hiding?

'Don't go telling anyone else I was in that courtyard,' he said, pointing his thin cigarette at her. 'Because it wasn't me.'

To Lottie's relief, they were interrupted by an announcement that Prince Manfred was going to make a speech. The announcement came from a man in a dark suit who'd appeared on a podium in the centre of the room. There was applause as Prince Manfred climbed up onto the podium and waved to his guests. He was accompanied by a slight man in a blue suit. As the prince spoke, Lottie realised he was talking in German. He spoke a sentence, then paused and waited as the blue-suited man translated his words into French. A long and stilted speech then followed about how grateful the prince was to be a patron of the arts and how much he liked Paris. Lottie thought of poor Mrs Moore who wouldn't be able to understand a word of it.

'Well, he talked an awful lot but said very little, didn't he?' said Tom once Prince Manfred had finished. Lottie agreed. 'I'd better circulate and see my friends now,' he said. 'Oh, one little thing before I go. Maddy's anxious about what people might think about our friendship in the light of what's happened. She's worried they might get the wrong idea. You'll look out for her at this difficult time, won't you?'

'Of course,' said Lottie, unsure of what else she could say.

'I knew it.' He tapped her on the shoulder and gave her a wink. 'I'll see you around.'

A flash of red in the corner of Lottie's eye signalled that Mrs Moore was heading towards her.

'Who were you talking to just then?'

'Tom Springer, he's the man I saw with Madeleine Lenoir.'

'Oh that's him! And they're just friends?'

'Apparently so.'

'Who's he with now?' She peered through her lorgnette to where Tom Springer was embracing a young woman in a gold dress. 'Do you think she's just a friend too?'

Chapter Fifteen

AT BREAKFAST THE FOLLOWING MORNING, Mrs Moore suggested a trip to Montmartre as suggested by Harriet Lenoir's gardien, Mr Boucher. A short while later, they found themselves at the foot of the Montmartre funicular railway, watching a carriage descend towards them.

'I'm not sure I want to go on this thing,' said Mrs Moore. 'What if it gets stuck?'

'I don't think it will,' said Lottie. She felt excited about climbing aboard.

'The cable might snap!'

'I'm quite sure it won't.'

'But how do you know that?'

'Well, I can't be completely certain, but I'm confident we'll be alright. Look, it's quite a clever system. One carriage goes up while the other comes down, then the first one comes down while the second goes up.'

'Clever is it? I'm going to close my eyes.'

'You'll miss the view!'

'I'll see the view when we're at the top. Or better still, perhaps I can climb the steps. Where are they?'

'Over there.' Lottie pointed to a flight of wide stone steps which led up the hill.

'Golly, I'm not climbing those. I'll have to get on this funny little train then.'

Lottie picked up Rosie and carried her into the carriage. They sat on a wooden slatted seat in front of a window. Lottie felt a thrill of delight as the carriage gave a jolt and began its slow climb to the top.

'Tell me when it's all over,' said Mrs Moore, sitting next to her with her eyes screwed shut.

Lottie smiled as the skyline of Paris came into view, the sun beamed down on the countless roofs and chimney tops.

'We're there,' said Lottie, as the carriage came to a halt.

'Already? How long was that? A minute?'

'And the cable didn't snap.'

'Shush, we haven't got out yet.'

THEY ADMIRED the view from a path at the top while Rosie sniffed at a lamppost. Behind them, another flight of steps led up to the white-domed church of Sacré-Cœur.

'It's disappointing that I only managed a brief conversation with Prince Manfred yesterday evening,' said Mrs Moore. 'And we had to speak through his interpreter, which slowed things down a little. I tell you what I need to do, Lottie, I need to learn German.'

'How?'

'I'll get a book on it. I don't expect to master the language, but some rudimentary knowledge of conversation should help me. He was very busy yesterday and I don't think he even remembered my name.'

'I'm sorry to hear it. He probably had a lot of people to talk to.'

'He did! There was practically a queue. Anyway, I think I managed to remind him who I was in the end and he let slip that he's been dining each evening at a restaurant called *Chez Florent*. So there's the solution, Lottie, we can dine there each evening too!'

After visiting the church, Lottie, Mrs Moore and Rosie explored the shops in Montmartre's little streets and Mrs Moore was overjoyed to find a copy of *Colloquial German* in a second-hand bookshop.

AFTER LUNCH, Mrs Moore sat down to study her new book while Lottie took Rosie to the Jardin des Tuileries. They hadn't been there long when a familiar black terrier scampered up to them.

'Edmond!' said Lottie. 'Who are you here with?'

It had been a pointless question because the dog was unable to answer. He and Rosie skipped off together while Lottie glanced around her.

It wasn't long before she saw someone she recognised: a man in a dark suit and boater hat, walking with the support of crutches. Next to him was a young woman in lemon yellow and holding a parasol.

Charles Lenoir greeted her as they approached. 'This is my fiancée, Florence,' he said. 'I'm afraid she doesn't speak much English.'

'That's quite alright, I can speak in French,' said Lottie.

'You can?' Charles raised an eyebrow. 'I didn't realise.'

Florence was slender with fair, wavy hair and large eyes like a doll. 'Lottie was with us when Jacques was murdered,' Charles explained to his fiancée. 'Not the sort of welcome we usually have for our guests. Have the police spoken to you, Lottie?'

'Only once. There wasn't much I could tell them.'

'I don't think there's much anybody can tell them. Apart from me, I suppose, because I found the poor chap.'

'Poor chap?' said Florence. 'I don't feel sorry for him.'

'I know he wasn't nice to you, but you still have to feel sorry for someone who was murdered.'

'I could happily have murdered him myself.'

Charles pulled a grimace and gave Lottie a sidelong glance. 'Don't let people hear you say things like that, Florence, otherwise they might suspect you had something to do with it.'

'No one will suspect me. Could they really believe that I would creep into your apartment and murder him? He wasn't worth the trouble. And besides, I have an alibi for the time, I was having dinner at my grandmother's house.'

'All I'm saying is you have to be careful about how you talk at times like this, Florence. People will hear things and then tell the police. Before you know it, you're having to explain yourself to them. And, believe me, you don't want to sit in front of Commissaire Gauthier, it's unnerving even when you know you're innocent. Self-doubt creeps in and you wonder if you've somehow murdered him by accident.'

'That's just silly,' said Florence 'How can you murder someone by accident?'

'I don't know how, but I'm sure it's happened. Sometimes in the heat of the moment when anger gets out of control...' He paused and rubbed his brow. 'I'm sorry, I don't know what I'm saying.'

'I suppose you could have murdered him on my behalf, couldn't you, Charles?'

'No, I wouldn't do anything like that.'

'But you stood up for me, didn't you? He was so horrible to me about my cats and you spoke to him about that.'

'Yes I did. I'm not sure he ever realised how much it upset you, but that was the sort of man he was.'

'So you didn't get on with him?' asked Lottie.

'I got on with him for the sake of my family. When he was visiting us, I did my best to make an effort and be polite. I didn't particularly want him to marry my sister, but I could see that it was... oh, don't worry about it.'

'Don't worry about what?' asked Florence.

'It's nothing.'

'It's not nothing. You were going to say something then.'

'Mother really wanted Maddy to marry him. I didn't want her to, but I had to go along with Mother's wishes. That's all there is to it. I suppose I should be pleased that the wedding is no longer happening. But it is a shame, especially for Maddy.'

'Who'd want to marry someone who kicks cats?' said Florence.

'He kicked your cats?'

'Not quite. But he shouted at them and told them to shoo.'

'That's still quite mean.'

'It's very mean. Perhaps Maddy decided she didn't want to marry him after all and she took matters into her own hands.'

'My sister is not a murderer.'

'Perhaps she did it by accident. You said yourself, Charles, that sometimes people get angry and out of control.'

'Maddy isn't capable of it.'

'Maybe she got someone to do it for her?'

'Like who?'

'Perhaps she paid someone to pretend to be a burglar?'

'Nonsense, Maddy wouldn't do something like that.'

'How do you know?'

'Because I know my sister.' Charles turned to Lottie. 'You have to excuse Florence, she has a fanciful imagination.'

'I don't think it's that fanciful,' said Lottie. 'Jacques could have been murdered by someone who knew him. There have been no sightings of the intruder yet, have there?'

'No there haven't.'

'And why did the burglar choose the drawing room?' asked Lottie. 'It's on the upper floor of the apartment. Why not choose to steal from a room nearest the entrance door?'

'I don't know,' said Charles. 'Perhaps there was someone nearby looking for Edmond?'

'There could have been someone looking for Edmond in any of the rooms,' said Lottie. 'I think the burglar took a risk by going up the stairs to the drawing room.'

'I can see your logic Lottie, but I think the burglar simply chose the most accessible room for him at that time. We know it was empty when he went in there because he had time to ransack some of the drawers. And then Jacques disturbed him.'

'It must have been someone already in the apartment,' said Florence.

Charles turned to her. 'Please stop accusing my family.'

'It could have been one of the servants.' Florence nodded at Lottie. 'And you also had guests that evening.'

'Lottie?' said Charles. 'I don't think so. And Roberta Moore wouldn't have done such a thing either.'

'It must be my fanciful imagination again,' said Florence.

'Yes, it must be,' said Charles. But his brow lowered, and he gave Lottie a look which made her feel uncomfortable.

Chapter Sixteen

TOM SPRINGER PICKED up his palette and smeared a little white paint onto his brush. Not too much, not too little. Then he applied the brush to the canvas and worked on the left edge of the bottle. He squinted hard as he worked, and his eyes felt sore.

Then he stood back and surveyed his work.

It was a mess. A chimpanzee would have done better.

He dropped the brush and the palette onto his cluttered table, sank onto his sofa and lit a cigarette. Could he save the picture? Or did he need to start all over again?

He couldn't start all over again because he was out of canvas and had no money to buy any more. He'd also run out of friends to ask for favours: all of them were owed money, cigarettes, drink, paint and canvas. If only he hadn't burned his parents' cheque! It had been stupid. So stupid. He thumped a fist down on the sofa cushion in frustration.

He'd burned the cheque because he'd accidentally destroyed it along with that letter. He'd done nothing about the letter yet, and he knew he should. But when? And how?

His mind returned to money. Maddy had told him she

could lend him some, but she'd appeared to have forgotten about it since her fiancé's murder. It was understandable, but he'd been surprised at how upset she was about Jacques's death. She hadn't even liked him!

It was enough to make him drink so much whisky that he could fall asleep and forget about everything. Life was so demanding! It felt exhausting.

A knock sounded at the door. He ignored it.

The knock sounded again.

'I'm not here!' he called out.

'Open the door!' A female voice. Speaking English. It didn't sound like Maddy. Was it that Lottie girl he'd spoken to last night? Had she found him irresistible and tracked him down? 'Open the door now!' The voice belonged to a woman older than Lottie. But who?

Curiosity got the better of him. He got up and opened the door.

'Mrs Lenoir?' He took a step back.

She wore a black coat over her plump frame and a black cloche hat. Her face was stern.

'May I come in?'

'Sure.' He staggered back into the room, his heart pounding. He'd never spoken to her before, he'd only seen her in the street when Maddy had pointed her out to him.

Mrs Lenoir's expression remained stony as she surveyed the room.

'Would you like to sit?' he gestured to his sorrowful sofa.

'No, thank you.' Her nose wrinkled. She didn't like what she saw, that much was obvious. He smoothed down his crumpled shirt and stubbed out his cigarette in the ashtray.

'How do you know—'

'About you? A friend told me. She saw you with Maddy. The pair of you should have been more discreet.'

'I'm er...' His mouth felt too dry to speak properly. 'I can explain...'

'You need to go back to America.' She stood directly in front of him, her hands on her hips.

'Go back? Why?'

'I need you as far away from my daughter as possible.'

'But we're just friends, there's nothing in it.'

'You must think I was born yesterday.'

'No, not at all. But if you want us to no longer be friends, then that's fine, it can be arranged.'

'I just need you to go back home.'

'I can't, Paris is my home now.'

'I will pay for your ticket.'

'Does Madeleine know you're here?'

'No. And there's no need for her to find out either.'

'I will stay away from her completely, you have my word. I know how this looks.' He gestured at his small, shabby apartment. 'But I know how to be a gentleman, even if I'm not one in the eyes of Parisian society. I'm an artist, I live on the periphery. I'm an honest man, Mrs Lenoir, and have always treated your daughter kindly. But I understand why you don't want me to be friends with her anymore—'

'I know you're more than friends!' She took a step towards him. 'And your continued presence here in Paris endangers my family.'

'How?'

'When the police learn of Maddy's relationship with you, they'll assume the pair of you are responsible for Jacques's death.'

'But we're not! It was an intruder!'

'That's what everyone thought at first, but the intruder can't be found. The police are going to consider other theories and they will ask more detailed questions. What do you think is going to happen if Jacques Marchand's family finds out about you?'

'I don't know, I hadn't thought about it.' But now he was thinking about it and he inwardly agreed they wouldn't be happy about his relationship with Maddy.

'Louis Marchand is a powerful man,' said Mrs Lenoir. 'And he's extremely upset about the death of his son. Imagine what he's going to think about my daughter if he discovers your relationship! I can't risk that happening. If you really love Madeleine, then you will leave Paris immediately. Her reputation needs to remain unsullied so she can marry well again in the future.'

The suggestion he wasn't good enough for Madeleine felt like a blow to Tom's chest.

'Perhaps if I'd studied mathematics or trained as a solicitor, then I would have been good enough.'

'I doubt it. The very best thing you can do for my daughter and my family now is to leave.' Mrs Lenoir opened her handbag and pulled out a handful of banknotes. 'Here's five hundred francs. That should be enough for a ticket in steerage to America.'

Tom took the money.

Mrs Lenoir snapped her handbag shut and made her way over to the door.

'I won't go,' he said. 'I can't go! People need me here!'

She turned. 'Like who?'

'Just... people. I will stay out of your daughter's way, Mrs Lenoir, I promise. But you cannot make me go back to America.'

'I've given you the money now, you have no excuse. And if you don't leave, then I shall tell the police.'

'Tell them what?'

'That you murdered Jacques Marchand. They're far more likely to believe me than you.'

Chapter Seventeen

AFTER HER CONVERSATION with Charles and Florence, Lottie made her way back to the hotel in a reflective mood. She hadn't warmed to Florence at all. Had she really suggested that Lottie or Mrs Moore could have murdered Jacques Marchand? It had been a ridiculous thing to say. And quite rude too, considering she didn't even know them. The more Lottie thought about it, the crosser she felt.

'What's happened?'

Lottie startled, she hadn't noticed Pierre the delivery boy wheeling his bicycle towards her.

'Nothing's happened.' She forced a smile.

'Are you sure? You're scowling.'

'I'm fine.'

'Good.' He grinned, propped his bicycle against a wall, and pulled a baguette out of the basket. 'Would you like some?'

'Aren't you supposed to be delivering it somewhere?'

'No one will notice if one is missing. I do it all the time.'

'Won't you lose your job?'

He laughed. 'You worry too much, Lottie.' He held out the bread for her and she ripped a piece off.

'Thank you.' The smell of fresh bread was mouth-watering.

'Still no sighting of the intruder,' said Pierre, pulling off a bit of baguette for himself. 'People are wondering if someone in the house carried out the crime.'

'And what do you think?'

'I think the Lenoir family is a bit... strange.'

'In what way?'

'It's difficult to explain. But I think they try to be more important than they are.'

'Do you think one of them is a murderer?'

'I don't know. But I do know that Madeleine Lenoir was spending time with that American artist behind Jacques Marchand's back. She was only marrying him for his money.'

'Which means she wouldn't murder him, would she? Because then she'd miss out on his money.'

'But she could have done if she considered love to be more important than money. If she's in love with the American, then perhaps she wanted to be rid of Jacques so she could marry him?'

'She seemed quite bored by Jacques, they didn't appear to have much in common.'

'So there you go. To her, maybe happiness is more important than money?'

'So much so that she'd murder for it?'

'Who knows?' He offered her another piece of bread. 'Who else is in that household? Charles Lenoir.'

'His fiancée, Florence, was once engaged to Jacques Marchand.'

'Was she?' He raised his eyebrows. 'Interesting! And who put an end to that?'

'Florence, I believe. He was mean to her cats.'

'That's not a nice way to behave. Why would someone even bother to be mean to cats?'

'Apparently, they made him sneeze, but that's not a suitable excuse.'

'No, it's not. So Charles could have been angered by Jacques being mean to his fiancée's cats and took revenge? Actually, I think it's more likely that the pair of them worked together. Florence urged Charles to do it because she was so upset about the cats.'

'I've just met her and there's no doubt she disliked Jacques after the relationship ended. But if she did wish him dead, then I'm sure there has to be a reason besides the cats.'

'Some people are very protective of their cats.' He took another bite of bread. 'What about Mrs Lenoir?'

'She wanted Madeleine and Jacques to marry, so I don't see why she would murder him.'

'All her plans have gone wrong, haven't they?'

'There's someone else we haven't considered, though.'

'Who's that?'

'Do you know the gardien in that apartment building, Mr Boucher?'

'You think he did it?'

'He's just someone else to consider.'

'I've met him a few times, he's new to the job. I speak with him when I'm delivering things.'

'He's adamant that he didn't see anybody coming or going on the night of the murder and he doesn't know how someone got in. It would be easy for him to have committed the crime though, wouldn't it?'

'Yes, it would! He was already in the building. But why would he try to steal from the Lenoir family while they had a dinner party in progress?'

'Maybe he was after Jacques Marchand.'

'But he would have barely known him.'

'How can you be sure? Perhaps the two did know each other and Mr Boucher isn't admitting to it?'

'What an interesting idea! If he is the murderer, then it was rather risky for him to enter the Lenoir's apartment. He could have been seen.'

'But he could have had an excuse prepared. He works in the building and could have made something up about checking water pipes or something similar.'

'He could have done.' Pierre chewed on another mouthful of bread. 'But here's what I think. If Mr Boucher is the murderer, then surely he would have made up a story that he saw an intruder coming or going? That would throw the police off the scent.'

'Yes, that would be a clever thing to do. It's difficult to lie that blatantly, though.'

'True. It takes a lot of courage to face a policeman and lie bare-faced. And the more of a story you construct, the more the details can be checked up on. I know that from experience.'

Lottie smiled. 'What have you lied about, then?'

'The number of baguettes I've delivered.' He laughed. 'Nothing worse than that. I've just had another idea! Maybe Mr Boucher isn't the murderer, but perhaps he let the murderer in and out of the building?'

'And agreed not to say anything?'

'Yes!'

'Perhaps the murderer bribed him to stay quiet?'

'He could have done. That's a thought.'

'How do you get to the courtyard at the back of the Lenoir's apartment building?'

'There's an alleyway on Rue Saint-Honoré.'

'Do you have time to show me?'

Pierre checked his watch. 'Very quickly. I need to get this bread delivered by four o'clock.'

Chapter Eighteen

'Why do you want to see the courtyard?' Pierre asked as he wheeled his bicycle alongside Lottie and Rosie.

'I saw a man there on the night of Jacques Marchand's murder, remember? I asked Tom Springer if it was him.'

'You asked him? Where did you see him?'

'At a preview of an art exhibition at the Grand Palais.'

Pierre gave an impressed whistle. 'You go to some fancy places. And Tom Springer was there too? What did he say when you asked him about it?'

'He denied it was him. And there's no way of proving it either. But I'd like to see where he was standing. And maybe if I stand in that same location myself, I might get an idea of what he was looking at.'

'You're becoming quite a sleuth!' He grinned.

They passed a boutique with expensive shoes in the window, then Pierre stopped by a narrow, cobbled passageway which ran between two buildings.

'Down here?' asked Lottie.

'Yes, but I won't come with you because I need to deliver this bread. Just watch out for Monsieur Soulier.'

'Who's he?'

'He owns the courtyard.'

'So I shouldn't go there?'

He laughed. 'Don't look so worried, Lottie! He probably won't see you.'

'But he might.'

'You'll be able to run faster than him. See you soon.' He gave her a wink, which made her face flush, and climbed onto his bicycle.

'Come on, Rosie,' said Lottie once Pierre had cycled away. 'Let's brave it.' The passageway was long and dingy, but she could see the sunny courtyard at the far end. She tried to calm her thudding heart as they walked. 'If we do see him, then we can just pretend we don't understand French and we're lost. Although you don't understand French anyway, so it only needs to be me who pretends.'

Eventually, Lottie and Rosie reached the courtyard, and she recognised the large tree, lamppost and bench which she'd seen from the study balcony. 'Tom Springer, or the man who looked like him, was standing right here,' she whispered to Rosie. Buildings bordered the courtyard on all four sides, and Lottie feared she was easy to spot from the countless windows. Many of them were shuttered, but there was a possibility the shutters had gaps which people might peek out of. She could only hope Monsieur Soulier wasn't one of them.

The building in front of her was the rear of the apartment block where the Lenoir family lived. She counted the floors and looked up at the balconies, wondering which one of them belonged to the study. There were two or three possibilities.

'Tom Springer had a good view of the building from here,' Lottie whispered to Rosie. 'But what was he doing here? Was he watching the windows? Or had he arranged to meet Madeleine here? Perhaps he was waiting for her to let him in at that door.'

The small blue door she could see was presumably the door which Mr Boucher had mentioned. He'd told her it had been locked. Lottie stepped over to it now and tried the handle. 'It's definitely locked, Rosie.'

Had Tom Springer arranged to meet Madeleine Lenoir that evening? And had she admitted him into the building through the blue door? Had the pair colluded to murder Jacques Marchand? It was a possibility, but Lottie couldn't fathom out how they could have managed it without being seen. Perhaps they'd just been lucky.

A raised voice startled her. There was no one else in the courtyard and she felt sure it had come from one of the windows. A few yards up from the door, she could see a shutter slightly ajar. She moved a little closer and strained her ears to listen.

A man spoke in French. 'Why are you doing this? You're ruining everything!'

It was Charles Lenoir, she felt sure of it. He must have returned from the park.

'I'm doing some people a favour.' It was Lucien Boucher's voice.

Lottie held her breath and listened some more.

'You shouldn't even be here,' said Charles.

'Since when do you decide where I can go?'

'You need to leave before things get even worse.'

'No, I'm quite happy staying where I am. People need to know the truth.'

'It doesn't matter anymore, it's irrelevant.'

Movement caught Lottie's eye, she turned to see a tabby cat stepping out from behind the tree. Rosie hadn't spotted it, instead she was sniffing at the base of the wall.

'That's where you're wrong,' she heard Lucien Boucher say. 'You're only a young man, one day you'll understand.'

'Don't condescend me! How can I make it easy for you? Do you want money?'

'I'm not accepting money from you.'

Rosie sniffed the air, then caught sight of the cat. Lottie willed her not to react. The cat stopped and stared, then arched its back, its fur lifting on end.

Please don't bark at the cat, Rosie, willed Lottie silently.

'If you won't go, I'll report you to the police,' said Charles.

Lucien laughed. 'But you know you can't, because I'm not the one who committed the crime! I'm afraid you just have to accept it, Mr Lenoir, there comes a time when people have to face their mistakes.'

Rosie stared at the cat and the cat stared at Rosie. Should Lottie shoo it away? That would make a noise in itself.

She heard Charles's voice next. 'But it's not fair on—'

He was interrupted by Rosie barking. Lottie's heart plummeted to her stomach. She scooped up her dog and dashed away from the window as quickly as she could. The cat scooted up the trunk of the tree.

'Whose dog is that?' came a voice behind her. She heard the shutter creak open and she knew Lucien and Charles would be watching her.

LOTTIE FELT her face burn with shame as she turned into Rue Saint-Honoré. She'd been caught eavesdropping. How could she explain herself? She clung onto a hope that neither of the men had recognised her, but it seemed unlikely.

She put Rosie down and tried not to feel cross with her for barking at the cat. Rosie always barked at cats, she couldn't help it. Lottie blamed herself for sneaking about in places she shouldn't be.

'Lottie!' Her heart thudded again. Was it Charles? No, it sounded like Pierre. She looked up and saw him cycling on the other side of the road. He got off his bicycle and crossed over to join her. The basket on the front of his bicycle was now empty.

'That was a quick delivery,' she said.

'It was only around the corner. So how did you get on?'

'Badly.'

'Monsieur Soulier saw you?'

'No, but I overheard a conversation between Charles Lenoir and Lucien Boucher.'

'Really? What were they talking about?'

'It seems that Charles doesn't want Lucien working there.'

'Why?'

'I don't know why, I wasn't able to listen for long enough to find out because Rosie barked at a cat and stopped the conversation. I ran off, but I heard the shutter open and they must have seen me.'

'Oh.'

'They know I was listening in to their conversation! It's so embarrassing.'

'If they ask you about it, you can say Rosie ran away from you into the courtyard and you went to fetch her.'

'That sounds believable enough.'

'It does, doesn't it? I'm quite good at coming up with excuses. Are you going back to your hotel now?'

'Yes. Mrs Moore will be wondering where I am.'

'Shall I take you back there?'

'Take me back? How?'

'You can hop on my bicycle. Just sit on the crossbar here in front of the saddle. When I'm holding the handlebars, my arms will keep you in position so you won't fall off. Rosie can go in my basket on the front.'

'It sounds a bit dangerous.'

'It's not! Come on, it'll be fun and you need cheering up. I've carried people on the crossbar lots of times.'

'Really?'

'Yes! You'll be back at the hotel in no time.' He climbed onto his bike. 'Let's go.'

'I'll have to see if Rosie's alright with the basket first.' Lottie picked up the dog and cautiously placed her in there. Rosie tidied up some crumbs in the base of the basket, then gave Lottie a contented glance with her large eyes. 'She looks quite happy.'

'Of course she's happy! Now just sit side-saddle on the crossbar in front of me.'

Lottie did so, aware of how close she was now to Pierre.

'Now I just put hands on the handlebars and my arms hold you there, is that alright?'

'Yes, I think so.' She felt a tingle at the back of her neck as his arms brushed either side of her. 'Is it safe?' she asked.

'Safe? Of course it's safe!' He pushed off with his feet and began to pedal. 'Wheeee!' He bounced the bicycle off the kerb and onto the road where a car beeped its horn at them. Pierre pedalled faster, then took a corner at exhilarating speed. Rosie poked her head out of the top of the basket and her tongue lolled happily out of her mouth.

'It's much more fun going through the park,' said Pierre, whizzing across the wide boulevard of Rue de Rivoli and entering the Jardin des Tuileries. Lottie felt a big smile on her face. The breeze whipped at her hair and she gripped the bicycle's crossbar so tightly that her palms hurt.

They sped along the wide, flat paths of the gardens. Pierre steered the bicycle expertly around pedestrians and perambulators then pedalled towards an ice cream stall before swerving away from it at the last minute. Lottie gave a shriek of delight, and an old man shook his walking stick at them.

'Shall we go around the pond?' said Pierre. Lottie giggled as the bicycle leaned to one side and they encircled the Grand

Basin Rond. The last time she'd been there was on a sedate walk with Madeleine Lenoir.

'Around again?' asked Pierre when they'd completed one circuit.

'Go on then!' laughed Lottie.

He pedalled faster this time, and the bicycle leaned even further. Lottie felt the wind in her ears and gripped the cross bar even tighter. It felt like the thrill of a fairground ride.

'Whoa!'

A pigeon flapped across their path. Rosie barked at it and it fluttered away unscathed.

'Time to get you back to the hotel,' said Pierre once he'd completed the second lap of the pond.

'No!' She didn't want the fairground ride to end.

'I'm exhausted!'

He slowed his pedalling as they navigated the paths back to Rue de Rivoli and the hotel. A few moments later, he stopped the bicycle outside it.

'Thank you Pierre, that was a lot of fun.'

'It was, wasn't it?' He grinned.

A hotel footman helped Lottie dismount. She lifted Rosie out of the basket, bid Pierre farewell, and watched him cycle away. Then she turned and made her way into the hotel, still giddy with excitement.

Chapter Nineteen

'GUTEN ABEND,' said Mrs Moore as they sat at a table in the restaurant *Chez Florent* that evening. 'Do you know what that means, Lottie?'

'Good evening?'

'It does indeed. You're a clever girl. Wie geht... oh, just a moment.' Mrs Moore opened her handbag, took out *Colloquial German*, and leafed through it. 'What is it again? Wie geht... I can't find it now. I learned it earlier and now I've forgotten it again! Anyway, it means "how are you", I shall have to look it up again later. I wanted to remember it so I could say it to Prince Manfred this evening.' She peered through her lorgnette at a nearby empty table which was set for eight. The waiter had informed them it was where the prince and his party would be sitting. 'He's going to be here shortly.' She grinned. 'Isn't that exciting, Lottie? We can speak to him! Well, through an interpreter, anyway. That's why I wanted to get some German learned this afternoon. Are you wearing rouge?'

'No.'

'Your cheeks must be quite flushed, then. You've looked

like that ever since you returned from your walk this after-noon. In fact, you were gone for quite a while. Where did you go?'

'Just the streets around the hotel and Jardin des Tuileries. I saw Charles Lenoir and his fiancée, Florence, there.'

'Did you? What's she like?'

'A bit rude.'

'Really? How disappointing. Charles seems like such a nice young man, too. Wie geht es Ihnen!'

'Sorry, what?'

'That's how you say "how are you" to someone in German. I remembered it! There's another way of saying it too, that's for when you're asking someone you know well. I can't remember what it is now. Oh golly, here he comes!'

An important-looking maître d' accompanied Prince Manfred to the table. He wore a red velvet jacket and a small velvet fez hat was perched on his head of dark curls. Once he'd taken his seat, seven more gentlemen joined him at the table. Lottie recognised one of them as the blue-suited man who'd acted as interpreter for the prince's speech at the art exhibition.

Mrs Moore gave the prince a little wave, and he returned it. 'Guten Abend!' she called out. He replied with a nod.

She turned excitedly to Lottie. 'Did you see that? He returned my wave, and he nodded.' She was grinning from ear-to-ear and her cheeks flushed redder than Lottie's.

The waiter came to their table and Mrs Moore turned her attention to the menu.

'Oh dear,' she said. 'My French isn't good, but this menu is making even less sense than usual.'

'You're holding it upside down,' whispered Lottie.

'Thank you,' she whispered in reply.

After they'd chosen their food, Mrs Moore glanced at the prince again and gave him another wave. 'My goal this evening is to join him at his table after dinner,' she said. 'Wouldn't that be nice? I suppose the other members of his party are advisers and assistants. I'm quite relieved there are no ladies at his table, that would worry me. As far as I'm aware, there are no ladies currently in the running to be his wife, so I've probably got as good a chance as anyone, wouldn't you say, Lottie? Anyway, I must calm myself. I feel like a frivolous young girl again.'

They dined on lobster bisque, followed by beef steak in a white wine sauce. 'Did Charles Lenoir have anything enlightening to say about recent tragic events?' asked Mrs Moore.

'Not really, although I overheard him having an argument with the gardien, Mr Boucher.'

'Where?'

'Rosie ran off from me down an alleyway.' Lottie didn't want to admit she'd been deliberately snooping. 'So I went after her and found her in the courtyard behind the Lenoir's apartment building.'

'What a coincidence!'

'It was. Then I heard a conversation between Charles and Mr Boucher through one of the windows and it sounded like Charles was accusing Mr Boucher of causing trouble. He asked him to leave and even offered him money.'

'Really?' Mrs Moore's eyes widened. 'But what could Lucien Boucher have done wrong? I like him!'

'Maybe Charles suspects Lucien Boucher murdered Jacques Marchand? Or maybe Lucien suspects Charles did it and has threatened to tell?'

'Or it could be about an unrelated matter,' said Mrs Moore. 'Perhaps Lucien was rude to one of Harriet's guests and Charles had a word with him about it. Whatever it is Lucien has done, it can only have recently happened because he's only been there for two weeks, hasn't he?'

'He said something about people having to face their mistakes.'

'Did he? I wonder what that can mean?' Mrs Moore took another sip of wine. 'It could mean just about anything. And you need to be careful about eavesdropping, Lottie, you'd be in trouble if you were ever caught.'

Laughter broke out at Prince Manfred's table, and Mrs Moore's attention was immediately diverted. Lottie's mind drifted to the wild bicycle ride through the gardens and found herself smiling. Pierre was a lot of fun, she hoped to bump into him again soon.

'He clearly has a wonderful sense of humour, doesn't he, Lottie?'

'Who?'

'Prince Manfred! Who else would I be talking about?'

'No one, obviously the prince.' She'd still been thinking about Pierre.

'I wish I could hear what he was laughing about.'

The waiter brought over two extravagant desserts piled high with fruit, cream and flakes of chocolate.

'Oh no, we didn't order these,' said Mrs Moore. 'In fact, we haven't even looked at the dessert menu yet.'

'These are served with the compliments of Prince Manfred,' said the waiter, gesturing at the Bavarian Prince.

'Gosh really?' Mrs Moore clasped a hand to her chest. 'We are truly honoured!' She turned to Prince Manfred's table. 'Thank you!'

He replied with a nod and a grin.

Mrs Moore picked up her long-handled dessert spoon. 'I should have learned German for thank you, shouldn't I? And I don't know about you, Lottie, but I think it's going to take me all night to eat this.'

Moments later, Prince Manfred's party got to their feet and left the restaurant.

Mrs Moore's spoon hung halfway between her dessert and her open mouth. 'He's just left? Just like that?'

Lottie didn't know what to say. The prince's sudden departure had certainly been a surprise.

'I thought we might be invited to his table,' said Mrs Moore sadly. 'Oh well.' She returned to her dessert. 'What a funny fellow, he really does play hard to get.'

Chapter Twenty

THE JAZZ BAND was in full swing at *Le Mystère* nightclub. People packed the dance floor, dancing energetically in a whirl of limbs, sequins and feathers. The floor was sticky with champagne, and the smell of tobacco smoke mingled with the scent of heady perfume.

Madeleine Lenoir sat with Tom Springer at a little round table in a darkened corner. She could barely see his face in the gloom, it was difficult to hear him over the jazz band too. They had to lean forward and shout into each other's ears.

'Who have you told about our relationship?' he asked.

'No one.'

'Are you sure?'

'Completely sure. Why?'

'Because your mother knows about us.'

'What?' Madeleine froze and held his gaze. 'How?'

'She told me one of her friends saw us together.'

'She *told* you that? You've spoken to her?'

'She visited my apartment.'

'*What*?' Madeleine couldn't believe what she was hearing. 'How did she know where you live?'

'I don't know.'

'Didn't you ask her?'

'No.'

'Why not?'

'I didn't get the chance. She's told me to leave.'

'Leave your apartment?'

'Leave Paris. Leave France, in fact, and go back to America.'

'What? *You can't*!'

'She told me my continued presence here endangers her family.'

'What nonsense! Why would she even say such a thing?'

'She doesn't want people to find out about our affair, especially not the Marchand family. And she wants you to keep your reputation intact so you can marry well in the future.'

Anger balled in Madeleine's chest. She was tired of her mother interfering in her life!

'And also it could look like you and I murdered Jacques to get him out of the way. The police could come calling at my door any day now.'

Madeleine felt sick. 'No!'

'As the police get more and more desperate to catch the killer, they're going to arrest just about anybody who had a motive. I'm an easy target, don't you see? I don't have money or status, I'm just a lowly artist. I'm an easy person to blame. Our affair isn't helping us, is it?'

'So you're going to do what she asked? And go back to America? *You can't leave*! What will happen to me? I will miss you so much I will die!' A sob erupted, and she couldn't hold back the tears any longer. Tom rested his hand on her arm.

'Don't get so upset, honey. All we have to do is pretend that I've left.'

'And how do we do that?' She could barely see him through the blur of her tears.

'You have to pretend to be really sad about something but refuse to say what it is. Then your mother will assume she's been successful in sending me away.'

'So you're not going anywhere?'

'I'll need to move to another apartment. I've been asking around and there's one in the 20th arrondissement.'

'But that's miles away! How will I get there?'

'I'm not sure yet, sweetie, but it's a darn sight nearer than America, isn't it? It's the best we can do.'

She felt a pain in her chest, as if her heart were breaking. 'But what if you get found out? Oh, I'm so worried we're going to be arrested now! It will be so difficult for us to see each other! Oh, it's so awful, how did it come to this?'

'Once a killer's been arrested, we'll be alright again, baby.'

'Baby? You've never called me that before.'

'Okay, I'll stick with honey.'

'Once a killer's been arrested, they'll forget about us, won't they?' said Madeleine.

'Exactly.' He patted her arm.

'And then you can move back to your apartment and everything will be the same as it was before?'

'Possibly.'

'Why only *possibly*?'

'I meant yes, it will be. Now listen, you're supposed to be a grieving fiancée, aren't you? Anything you can do to convince the police that you're desperately upset about Jacques's death will help you.'

'Alright.' She dabbed her eyes and hoped the tears hadn't made her eyeliner run.

'Where does your mother think you are now?'

'With my friend Chloe.'

'Right, well, keep up the pretence. Hopefully, it won't be for much longer.'

'And when they get the murderer, we can be free!' She

leaned closer to him and cradled his face. 'Free to do what we like! I can move into your apartment with you!'

'Let's discuss that once the murderer is found.' He gently removed her hands from his face.

She sensed reluctance. 'Don't you want me to?'

'Of course I do, baby! I mean, honey. It's just that... a lot has happened in the past few days and your mother's visit gave me a fright.'

'I'm not surprised.'

'Come on, let me find you a taxi.'

'But it's only ten o'clock!'

'You're supposed to be a grieving fiancée. You should be moping around at home.'

'Alright.' She reluctantly got to her feet. 'Will I see you tomorrow?'

'Maybe.'

'Why only *maybe*?'

'I have to move to my new apartment. I'll send you a telegram when we can meet.'

'And what are you going to do now?'

'I'm going to go back to my apartment to pack up my things.'

'I can help you!'

'No, it's best you go home.'

'Why can't I come with you?'

'We can't be seen together, can we? I'm supposed to be going to America.'

She felt like she was being rebuffed and she didn't like it. Tom wasn't usually like this. 'You don't want me to come with you.'

'Yes I do. But it's not sensible right now, Ameli...'

'What did you just call me?'

'Maddy.'

'No you didn't, you were about to say another name!'

'No I wasn't! You're imagining things now. Listen, I'll send you a telegram as soon as I've moved.'

'Tomorrow?'

'Tomorrow.' He was avoiding her gaze.

'Are you keeping something from me?' she asked.

'No, why do you think that?'

'Because you almost said someone else's name. And you seem different.'

'Honey, I swear right now that I'm not keeping anything from you. This is just a difficult time. But we'll be fine, won't we?' He gave her a wink.

Could she trust him? She thought she did but she wasn't sure now. She'd assumed life would be easier without Jacques around, but it was turning out to be worse.

It was eleven o'clock when the taxi deposited Lottie and Mrs Moore at the hotel. 'Look at that!' said Mrs Moore, pointing up at the sky. 'A full moon tonight! Isn't it bright? You could turn off all the street lights and still find your way.'

They were approaching the hotel steps when they were startled by the screeching sound of bicycle brakes.

'Mind where you're going, young man!' said Mrs Moore.

'Lottie,' said a breathless Pierre. 'I was just coming to find you.'

'You know this gentleman?' Mrs Moore asked Lottie.

'Yes. He's Pierre. He's a delivery boy.'

'Who almost knocked us over! What's he saying?'

'It's fine. He always cycles about like that.'

'Something terrible's happened,' said Pierre. 'It's Lucien Boucher. He's dead.'

'LUCIEN BOUCHER WAS MURDERED in his apartment,' said Pierre. 'The housekeeper for the Picard family knocked at his door but there was no answer. She realised the door was unlocked, she opened it and she found him. That's what a police officer told me.' He paused to allow Lottie to translate this for Mrs Moore. Then he continued, 'They think he was hit with something heavy, just like Jacques Marchand.'

'Another intruder?' said Lottie. 'Or someone trying to make it look like an intruder?'

'I've told you all I know. But I don't see why a burglar would target the gardien of an apartment building,' said Pierre. 'A gardien doesn't usually have belongings worth stealing.'

'Spare keys to the apartments?' said Lottie. 'They would be worth stealing. Or perhaps Lucien Boucher had something valuable which the thief knew about?' She thought about this for a moment. 'Or maybe it wasn't a thief at all. Perhaps it's the same person who murdered Jacques Marchand.'

'But what can Jacques Marchand have in common with Lucien Boucher?' said Pierre.

'Charles Lenoir.'

'Charles did it?' said Mrs Moore.

'He's the only connection I can think of between Jacques and Lucien,' said Lottie. 'And I heard a disagreement between Charles and Lucien this afternoon.'

'You're going to have to tell the police about it, Lottie,' said her employer.

'But if Charles is innocent, then it looks like I'm causing trouble for him.'

'And if he's not, you're helping the police catch a murderer.'

LOTTIE STRUGGLED to sleep that night. Moonlight peeked in through the gap between the curtains, giving her room an eerie glow. Her mind whirled with thoughts of Lucien Boucher's murder. Could Charles Lenoir really have killed him?

The harder she tried to calm her thoughts, the more difficult it became. 'I give up,' she muttered, climbing out of bed. She pulled on her shabby woollen dressing gown and took her notebook out of the dressing-table drawer. Then she pulled open the curtains and moonlight streamed in through the window. Outside, the city bathed in peaceful, pale light.

Rosie stirred and lifted her head. She'd been sleeping at the end of Lottie's bed. 'Sorry I woke you up,' Lottie whispered. But the dog didn't seem to mind, she rested her head on her paws and gave Lottie a watchful gaze.

The moonlight was bright enough to write by. Lottie sat at the dressing table and opened her notebook and made some notes.

APRIL 8TH

Midday - we went on a boat trip with Harriet Lenoir, Madeleine Lenoir, Charles Lenoir and Jacques Marchand.

6.00 pm (approx.) - I saw Madeleine Lenoir with Tom Springer, they passed me in the street.

APRIL 9TH

We had dinner with the Lenoir family.

9.20 pm - I saw a man resembling Tom Springer waiting in the courtyard behind the apartment building.

9.30 pm - Jacques Marchand was found dead in the drawing room. Charles Lenoir discovered him.

APRIL 10TH

11.00 am (approx.) - I bumped into Madeleine in Jardin des Tuileries. She asked me not to mention Tom to anyone.

Evening - Tom Springer spoke to me at the art exhibition and asked me not to mention his and Madeleine's 'friendship'.

APRIL 11TH

4.00 pm - I overheard Charles Lenoir and Lucien Boucher arguing. Charles asked Lucien to leave because he was causing trouble and Lucien told him people have to face up to their mistakes.

11.00 pm - we found out Lucien Boucher was murdered in his apartment. Exact time of murder not yet known.

LOTTIE CHEWED on the end of her pen, then turned to Rosie. 'I thought writing it all down would help,' she whispered. 'But I don't think it's helped at all.'

∼

AFTER BREAKFAST THE FOLLOWING MORNING, Lottie, Mrs Moore and Rosie walked to the Lenoir family's apartment building. The sky was grey and overcast.

'I still can't believe someone would murder Lucien Boucher!' said Mrs Moore. 'With Jacques Marchand, I could understand it. Oh dear, does that sound unreasonable? I think you know what I mean, though, Lottie. That young man was rather strange and I'd barely conversed with him, so I didn't really know him. But Lucien! I realise I didn't know him either, but we had a couple of pleasant conversations and he was perfectly charming. I just can't fathom it at all!'

A police officer guarded the building, he wore a flat, round cap and a cape. A man with a notebook was asking him questions, but the policeman refused to respond.

Lottie told the policeman she had some information about Mr Boucher and asked to speak to Commissaire Gauthier.

'You may go inside,' he replied. 'Speak to one of my colleagues and they will find him for you.'

'Can I go inside?' asked the man with the notebook.

'No, because you are a nuisance.'

'I'm a news reporter!'

'And a nuisance.'

Mrs Moore and Rosie were allowed into the lobby with Lottie. She spoke to another police officer, and was told to wait for the commissaire.

The door to Mr Boucher's apartment stood open and two police officers were having a discussion in the doorway.

Mrs Moore surveyed the scene through her lorgnette. 'How do you think the intruder got into his apartment?' she whispered to Lottie. 'Do you think he broke in or Lucien let him in?'

'It would be interesting to find out,' said Lottie. 'If he let him in, that suggests he knew him or trusted him.' *Would he have let in Charles Lenoir?* Lottie wondered.

'I wonder how poor Harriet is,' said Mrs Moore. 'Another murder in her apartment building! Just dreadful. I wonder if she saw anything?'

'I expect the police will be speaking to her again.'

'Yes, they will, as if she hasn't had enough of them already!'

The police officers in the doorway of Mr Boucher's apartment stepped aside to allow the thick-set frame of Commissaire Gauthier to pass through. He strode over to Lottie and Mrs Moore, puffing on his pipe. 'You need to tell me something?'

His brusque manner encouraged Lottie to get her story out as quickly as possible. He clearly had little time on his hands.

'So you're telling me that Lucien Boucher exchanged cross words with Charles Lenoir yesterday afternoon and that you overheard their conversation while you were in the courtyard at the back of the building,' he summarised.

'Yes, that's right.'

'And what were you doing in the courtyard?'

'I had to fetch my dog.' She felt a tickle in her throat as she repeated the white lie she'd told Mrs Moore.

'You asked Monsieur Soulier's permission?'

'Erm... no. I didn't realise I had to.'

'So you were trespassing?'

'I suppose I was, yes. But I had to fetch my dog.'

The commissaire wrote something in his notebook.

'So you were by the window and you saw Lucien Boucher and Charles Lenoir?'

'I didn't see them.'

'So how do you know it was them?'

'I heard them. I recognised their voices.'

'You knew them well enough to recognise them by their voices alone?'

'Not very well. But I'd had conversations with both of them and I'm quite sure I recognised their voices.'

'They spoke in French?'

'Yes.'

'And you are English. I know your French is quite good, but it is possible you may have misheard some of the conversation as you translated it in your mind.'

He seemed keen to cast doubt on Lottie's story. 'I suppose there's a slight possibility. But I know what I heard!' she said. 'And I'm just trying to help.'

He gave a nod. 'But you cannot prove it was those two gentlemen that you heard. And you only heard part of the conversation, so we don't know exactly what they were talking about. Other than that, I suppose it could be interesting to us. Thank you for your time.'

He folded up his notebook.

'Can we visit Harriet Lenoir?' Mrs Moore asked.

'She's speaking to my colleagues at the moment. All the residents are being spoken to. I can pass on a message if you want.'

'Can you let her know that Mrs Moore called on her, please?'

'Very well.' He walked off and Lottie decided he hadn't been particularly interested in what she'd told him.

'He's quite sour-faced, isn't he?' said Mrs Moore.

'He's probably annoyed the murderer has struck a second time.'

THEY TURNED and headed for the door. As they did so, two small scraps of white by the skirting board caught Lottie's eye. She stopped and saw two pieces of paper which had presumably been blown against the wall by the draught from the main door.

Bending down, Lottie picked up the two scraps. Their edges were torn, as if they were the remains of something which had been ripped up. Lottie put them in the pocket of her skirt.

'What have you just picked up off the floor, Lottie? You'll get germs on your hands!'

'Just something which looked interesting.'

'If it's interesting, then perhaps you should hand it to the police?'

'I don't think they'll be bothered about it. It's probably nothing.'

Chapter Twenty-Two

'I CAN'T TELL you how nice it is to be out of that apartment building, Roberta,' said Harriet Lenoir. She dipped a slice of bread into her onion soup. 'It's been practically intolerable!'

They were lunching in the hotel restaurant and Lottie sipped at her soup before realising she'd picked up the wrong spoon for it.

'I can't imagine how awful it must be for you, Harriet,' said Mrs Moore.

'I expect you're wishing now that we'd never bumped into each other in the Jardin des Tuileries!'

'No, not at all! Why do you say that?'

'Because I invited you to my home where someone decided to murder my future son-in-law while we had dinner! You were all set to enjoy yourself here, Roberta, and now your fun has been ruined. It wouldn't surprise me if you decided to have nothing else to do with me.' Mrs Lenoir sighed. She wore a black dress and had dark circles beneath her eyes. Lottie noticed how different she was to the lady in peachy-pink who'd waved to them from the gleaming white boat just a few days previously.

'Of course I'll have everything to do with you, Harriet. Everything must be so difficult for you at the moment. Just as you were trying to cope with Jacques's murder, someone attacked and killed the gardien in your apartment building!'

'I can't comprehend it. And it has to be the same person. Both of them were hit over the back of the head with something heavy. The police told me that Mr Boucher's killer used a paperweight from his writing desk.'

'How awful!'

Lottie listened to the conversation and wondered if she should wipe her spoon clean with her serviette and pick up the correct one. Or could she continue with the wrong one? Mrs Moore seemed too engrossed in the conversation to notice.

'Do you mind if I confess something to you, Roberta?'

'No, not at all!' Mrs Moore's eyes grew wide with interest.

'I've discovered a few things about my family which are most distressing,' said Mrs Lenoir. 'And there are few people I can talk to about them.' She pulled out a handkerchief. 'If Antoine were still here, then he would have been a superb help, but sadly he isn't. Oh how I miss him, I'm quite sure we wouldn't be in this mess if he were still here.'

'I'm sorry to hear it, Harriet.'

'You probably realise, Roberta, that there's a need to maintain a certain image here in Paris. I became particularly conscious of that as I organised Maddy's wedding. I wanted to pretend everything was perfect. But the truth is, no family is perfect, is it?'

'Sadly not.'

'Do you promise to keep what I'm about to tell you in your strictest confidence?'

'Of course, Harriet.'

Mrs Lenoir didn't ask Lottie, it was probably assumed she would be discreet.

'A couple of weeks ago, a friend informed me that Maddy

had been seen about town with a young gentleman. A young gentleman who was not her fiancé.'

'No!'

'I'm afraid so. It was the very last thing I expected to hear, and it took me a few days to even believe it. I didn't want to believe it and I'm afraid I buried my head in the sand a little. I was exceptionally keen for Maddy to marry Jacques Marchand and I knew she wouldn't be marrying him entirely for love. Money was also important.'

'Absolutely, I understand.'

'I didn't ask Maddy directly about the young gentleman she'd been seen with because I worried she would use the conversation as an opportunity to convince me why she shouldn't marry Jacques Marchand. I didn't want anything to scupper the marriage, so I pretended I knew nothing of the affair and continued to organise the wedding as well as I possibly could. I wanted to charge onwards, like a heavy great steam engine.'

'And I can quite understand why, Harriet.'

'I did it all for Maddy.' Her voice began to crack. 'Her marriage to Jacques would have set her up with everything she possibly needed. Anyway, now that Jacques is dead, I suppose people will ask questions about who wanted him dead. And the police might look at Madeleine!' She wiped her eyes.

'No! She couldn't have done that to her own fiancé!'

'I don't think she could either, but the police might see it differently if they find out about the affair. It's important it remains completely secret. So I paid a visit to the young man yesterday and asked him to leave.'

'Who is he?'

'An American who goes by the name of Tom Springer. He claims to be an artist, but so do many people in Paris at the moment who are too lazy to earn an honest living.'

Mrs Moore tutted. 'I know the sort.'

'Anyway, he's left now.'

'Where's he gone?' asked Mrs Moore.

'To America. I gave him money for a ticket.'

'You paid for his ticket?'

'Only in steerage, he doesn't appear to have much money of his own. You should see the state of his apartment. I can only hope he hasn't been asking Maddy for money.'

'And you're sure now that he's gone?'

'I can't be certain, but Maddy is upset about something and has shut herself in her room. She won't talk to me about it and that suggests to me that he's gone. In fact, she seems far more upset about him going back to America than she does about the death of her fiancé.'

'Well, it sounds like you've done the right thing, Harriet. As you say, Madeleine needs to marry well and I don't think her father would have been proud of her running around with a chap like Tom Springer.'

'I only ever tried to do what I thought was best.' She emitted a sob.

'Of course you did, Harriet.'

'And it's all gone so wrong. To think I found someone suitable for her and now he's dead!'

'And Mr Boucher?'

'What about him?'

'He's also dead. I was telling Lottie earlier about how upsetting I find it. He was a charming gentleman.'

'I didn't know him. Obviously, I encountered him now and again and it's awfully sad he's been murdered.'

Lottie wondered if she knew her son had argued with Mr Boucher. Had Charles told her?

'I just can't think who's carrying out these awful attacks,' said Mrs Lenoir. 'Who's next?'

'Oh what a thought!' said Mrs Moore. 'You mustn't think like that Harriet, it's simply too terrifying!'

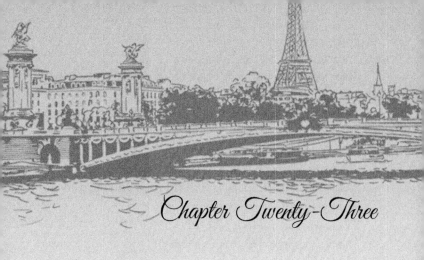

Chapter Twenty-Three

'When did you last see Mr Boucher?' asked Commissaire Gauthier. He sat opposite Charles on a yellow armchair in the sitting room and puffed on his pipe.

Charles thought back to the last time he'd seen him. He couldn't mention that, so it had to be the time before. When had it been?

'Yesterday afternoon,' he said. 'I saw him in the lobby when I returned from a walk in Jardin des Tuileries with my fiancée, Florence.'

'Was Florence with you?'

'No, we'd parted ways by then. Not permanently!' He gave a little laugh to ease the tension. 'Just for the day.'

'So what time did you see Mr Boucher in the lobby?'

'About a quarter-past-three.'

'Did you speak to him?'

'I wished him a good afternoon as far as I can recall.'

'And how did he seem?'

'His normal self. He was polite.'

'How well did you know Mr Boucher?'

'Not well at all, he'd only been working here for about two weeks.'

'What did you do after you wished Mr Boucher good afternoon?'

'Came up here to our apartment.'

'Did you see anyone when you arrived here?'

'I saw my mother briefly and then I went into the study to catch up with some correspondence.'

'Were you there at four o'clock?'

'I believe so, yes.' His mouth felt dry.

'You believe so, or you know so?'

'I believe so. I wasn't exactly watching the clock, I was immersed in my work.'

'So you can't say for certain that you were in the study at four o'clock?'

What was the man getting at? What did he know? Charles gritted his teeth and remained patient. 'I was working in the study for a while and I'm certain I was there at four and for some time after that, too.'

The commissaire consulted his notebook and scratched at his temple. 'I have reason to believe you had a conversation with Mr Boucher at four o'clock.'

So the English girl had talked after all! He stifled a sigh. What had she been doing snooping on the other side of the window? He and Lucien had spoken in French. How much French did she understand? What had she heard? He couldn't be sure. He tried to calm himself and appear relaxed.

'I remember now, I did. I had to speak to him about a broken light on the stairwell.'

Cold perspiration broke out on his forehead. He'd just told a lie to a senior police officer.

'You spoke to him about a broken light? Where did this conversation take place?'

'There's a storage room on the ground floor at the back of the building. I found him in there.'

'And did you speak to him about anything else?'

'No, that was all.'

The detective gave him a searching look, as if waiting for Charles to tell him something else. He felt the need to fill the silence. 'And then I... went back upstairs to my study.'

'Why didn't you inform me of the conversation about the broken light earlier? Did you simply forget or did you omit it on purpose?'

'I forgot! It's been a very difficult few days, as you can imagine, and something as ordinary as a broken light is the sort of thing that's quickly forgotten about. I do apologise.'

'And you're sure you discussed nothing else in your conversation? You didn't ask Lucien Boucher to leave?'

The English girl had heard more than he'd realised. He gave an awkward laugh. 'Actually I did.'

'You did?'

'Yes. I have to admit that I was annoyed with him for not having fixed the broken light sooner. It wasn't the first time we'd had to speak to him about it.'

'You'd spoken to him about it before?'

'I hadn't... but I believe my mother and sister had. One or both of them, I can't quite remember.' His palms were damp, and he knew his words sounded ridiculous. 'Anyway, I was annoyed about the light and I suggested he should leave his job because he wasn't doing it very well. I was a little angrier than I should have been and I regret that now.'

'Apparently, he told you that people had to face their mistakes.'

'Exactly, yes. He had to face his mistake of not getting the light fixed sooner.'

The commissaire gave a slow nod. Was it possible that Charles's muddled explanation was enough? 'I apologise again for not mentioning this conversation sooner,' he continued. 'My head is muddled at the moment. Just a few days ago, I happened to discover the body of Jacques Marchand, which is a terrible shock to a chap like me. You police officers are used to dealing with this sort of thing, but I've never come across anything like it.'

'Not even during the war?' The commissaire glanced at his missing leg.

Charles sighed. 'I prefer to forget about the war. Yes, horrible things happened then too. But the murder was in our family home! You must understand that's quite different. My mother or sister could have been killed! And for the attacker to have struck again in this very building... I find it extremely upsetting. So I'm sorry if my answers have been a little confused, Commissaire, but I must say I'm in a troubled state of mind at the moment.'

'Of course. I understand, Mr Lenoir, it's been a difficult few days for you.'

'But what are you doing about this man? He's broken into this building twice now and murdered two innocent people! What are you doing to find him?'

'We're doing our best, Mr Lenoir.'

'Are you sure? Because sitting here firing questions at me isn't going to help you catch him, is it?'

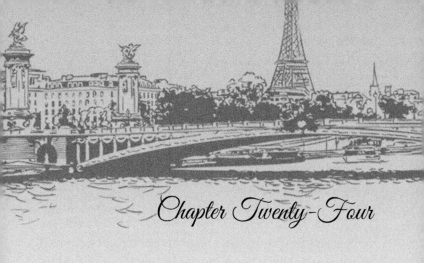

Chapter Twenty-Four

'HARRIET LENOIR HAS WORN ME OUT,' said Mrs Moore once her friend had left the hotel. 'It can be quite exhausting listening to other people's problems, can't it? I'm going to need a lie down this afternoon so I can prepare for our meal this evening with Prince Manfred.'

'We're dining with him?' asked Lottie.

'Not quite, we'll be sitting at a table close by again. Hopefully, we'll have an opportunity to sit with him. I don't know why he dashed off so suddenly last night. I must remember to learn a few more German phrases before this evening, too.'

'I'll take Rosie for a little walk.'

'Just a little walk?' Mrs Moore's eyes narrowed.

'Yes.'

'You're not going to go snooping again, are you, Lottie? You need to be careful. There's a very dangerous person out there.'

'I'm going to take Rosie for a walk and that's all.'

'Alright then, I shall see you later. And don't be too long, we need to get to *Chez Florent* in good time this evening.'

. . .

As she made her way along Rue de Rivoli, Lottie remembered the two scraps of paper she'd picked up from the floor of the lobby in the Lenoir's apartment building. Looping Rosie's lead around her wrist, she pulled them out of her pocket and examined them. The smaller piece contained a fragment of a word: "ing". The larger piece looked more interesting, it had an address on it: "8 Rue Legouvé". Was it an address in Paris? Or was it elsewhere in France? Lottie wondered how she could find out.

She put the scraps of paper into her pocket and continued on her way. As she walked, she mulled over Harriet Lenoir's conversation at lunchtime. Mrs Lenoir's frankness about her family had been surprising. She was a lady who clearly worked hard to present a respectable image, so why had she admitted her family's problems to Mrs Moore? And were there any clues in the things she'd told them?

Lottie's thoughts about the Lenoir family had unwittingly led her on the route to their apartment building. Realising where she was, she paused before she reached their home. She didn't want to be caught snooping again. She stood by a bar called *Le Canard Rouge* where Rosie greeted a poodle. The grey sky was growing darker and Lottie felt a spot of rain on her cheek. Then a young woman in an ice blue dress and matching hat stepped out of the Lenoir's apartment building.

Madeleine Lenoir.

Would Madeleine accuse Lottie of snooping if she saw her? Lottie hoped not, they were supposed to be friends. She decided to speak to her and find out what she thought about Mr Boucher's murder.

'Lottie!' Madeleine greeted her with a smile. 'How nice to see you!' She patted Rosie on the head.

'I heard about Lucien Boucher,' said Lottie. 'How are you?'

Madeleine's face fell. 'It's awful! And it's all the police's fault! If they'd caught the man who killed Jacques, then he wouldn't have been free to do it again, would he? It's really quite horrible. Mother and I were talking just now about how our fortunes have changed. This time last week, I was all set to marry Jacques. And now he's dead! Anyway, I'm just going out for a little walk. I would invite you to join me, Lottie, but I would like some time to myself. I hope you understand? It's been another very difficult day.'

'Of course. Enjoy your walk, Maddy.'

Lottie watched her head towards Rue de Rivoli, wishing she'd found the opportunity to ask her about Tom Springer. How upset was she by his departure for America?

'Shall we go to the park?' she asked Rosie. The corgi looked up at her with her large eyes. 'I'll assume you said yes.'

The route would take her the same way as Madeleine Lenoir. She followed her, keeping the ice blue dress in sight.

Once they reached the Rue de Rivoli, Lottie paused to cross the road. Madeleine wasn't crossing the road, instead she was walking briskly along the boulevard. Then she held out her hand and hailed a shiny blue taxi.

'I thought she was going for a walk?' Lottie said to Rosie.

The taxi stopped, facing them. It was close enough for Lottie to read the number plate beneath its tall radiator grille. She watched as it turned around in the road and headed off in the opposite direction.

Lottie jogged after the car, hoping to see where it would go. It didn't get far, it had to stop at a junction and wait as a policeman directed traffic.

'If only we could follow it and find out where Maddy's going,' Lottie said to Rosie. 'I want to know why she lied about going for a walk.' Lottie would have liked to hail a taxi, but she didn't have enough money for one. Then she had another idea. They weren't far from the bakery. Could Pierre be there with his bicycle?

'Come on!' She turned down a side street, then dashed around the corner, dodging pedestrians as she went. She grinned as she saw Pierre's bicycle propped up outside the bakery.

Inside the bakery, the aroma of fresh bread made her stomach grumble. Pierre leaned against the counter, twiddling a pencil between his fingers.

'Lottie?' He gave her a handsome grin.

'Can I borrow your bicycle?'

'What for?'

'I need to follow someone.'

'Who?'

'I haven't got time to explain, I'm going to lose them.'

He glanced at the door at the back of the shop, presumably wondering where the baker was. 'I'll come with you.'

'Are you sure?'

'Yes, we'll only be quick, won't we?'

'I hope so.'

They both rushed out into the street. 'You sit on the crossbar and I'll pedal. Rosie's alright in the basket, isn't she?'

'Rosie loves the basket.'

They were soon ready. 'Where are we going?'

'Rue de Rivoli. We need to follow a taxi.'

As Pierre rounded the corner into the boulevard, Lottie cautiously released a hand from the crossbar and pointed in the direction she'd last seen the taxi. 'It must have gone that way, but I can't see it now.'

'This is a busy road, it won't have been able to move very quickly. Who are we following?'

'Madeleine Lenoir. I saw her get into a taxi when she told me she was going for a walk.'

'She lied?'

'Yes. Very suspicious!'

Pierre weaved around a bus and Lottie clung on tight,

eagerly looking for a taxi. 'There it is!' she said. 'No it's not. It's a different number plate.'

'You can remember the registration number?'

'It begins with 63, that's all I can remember. There it is!'

They were alongside the wall of the Louvre Museum which had a long row of arched windows and statues in curved recesses.

'Don't get too close in case she turns around and sees us,' said Lottie. The taxi had a window at the rear, and she was fearful of seeing Madeleine's face peering out of it.

They continued along the wide, straight road and the taxi crossed over tram lines at the junction with Rue de Pont Neuf.

'Watch out!' cried Lottie as they passed in front of a green tram. It sounded its bell.

Rosie's tongue lolled as she watched the scenery pass by. They passed an elaborate tall church tower, about five storeys high. 'What's that?' asked Lottie.

'Tour Saint-Jacques,' said Pierre. 'The rest of the church was destroyed in the Revolution. I wonder where Madeleine is going?'

'I can't wait to find out. I can only hope we manage to keep up with her.' They passed a horse and cart, then stopped at a junction. Lottie prayed Madeleine wouldn't turn to look at the road behind and spot them. Then they were off again and a grand, symmetrical building with intricate windows and carved stonework caught her eye. 'That looks like a palace,' said Lottie.

'It's the city hall,' said Pierre. 'Are you sightseeing or watching the taxi?'

'Can't I do both?' she laughed.

They bumped over more tramlines and overtook a delivery van which honked its horn at them. The boulevard narrowed a little, and the buildings were less grand now. They passed cafes and restaurants and reached a vast square. In its centre was a tall column with a gold statue on top.

'This is Place de la Bastille,' said Pierre. 'Lots of roads lead from here, let's see which way she goes.'

They followed the taxi on a wide, curving road around the monument, and then headed into a narrow street lined with shops and restaurants.

'Now we're going northeast.'

'How do you know that?'

'I just do. And it's uphill too. Oh no, it's beginning to rain!'

The raindrops pattered on Lottie's hat and her blouse and skirt grew damp. They left the shops and restaurants, and entered a residential area with trees and apartment blocks of cream stone.

'How long is this journey going to take?' asked Pierre. He was panting now, and Lottie thought it would be unfair to expect him to cycle for much longer.

'Where are we?' she asked.

'The 20th arrondissement I think.'

It meant little to Lottie. She scanned the road ahead and her heart sank.

'I can't see the taxi anymore. It's gone.'

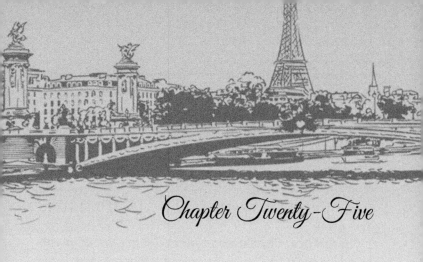

Chapter Twenty-Five

'IT'S GONE?' Pierre stopped pedalling, and Lottie climbed off the bicycle. 'Where?'

'I don't know. It must have turned off somewhere.'

'You didn't see where?' said Pierre between puffs. His face was red. He took off his cap and wiped away the damp hair which stuck to his forehead.

'No. But it can't have gone far!'

Lottie glanced around. The rain was falling steadily now. They were close to a junction where they could have turned either left or right. On the other side of the junction stood a tall wall with a gate. 'Is that a park?' asked Lottie.

'It's Père Lachaise cemetery,' said Pierre, putting his cap back on.

Lottie walked up to the junction and Pierre followed, wheeling his bicycle with Rosie still in the basket. Lottie looked up and down the road. It was quiet and lined with trees and apartment buildings.

'Left or right?' asked Pierre.

'I don't know. Right. No. Left.'

They walked a short distance to the left and there was no sign of the taxi.

'My bicycle has developed a squeak,' said Pierre.

'I can hear it. Did it not do that before?'

'No, it's just started, it's going to—'

'There it is!' They watched as the taxi passed them. The rear window revealed the passenger seat was empty. 'He's dropped Madeleine off somewhere around here!' said Lottie. 'But where?'

'Is that her?' He pointed to where a couple stood beneath a black umbrella further up the street. Lottie recognised the ice blue of the dress immediately.

'Yes! Who's she with?' The man wore a pale suit. 'Could it be Tom Springer? I heard he was going back to America.'

'Where did you hear that?'

'From Harriet Lenoir. She paid for his ticket home.'

'Really?' Pierre laughed. 'It doesn't look like he's on his way back to America, does it?'

'Unless he's going tomorrow and they're saying a final farewell.'

'They might see us,' said Pierre. 'Let's step back behind this tree.'

They did so and watched as Madeleine and Tom crossed the road and made their way toward the cemetery gates.

'They're going for a walk in the rain,' whispered Lottie. 'Should we follow them?'

'Yes. I haven't cycled three miles just to go back to the bakery again.'

'Will the baker be expecting you soon?'

'Yes, I should go back soon. But I have a bit of time.'

Madeleine and Tom walked through the cemetery gates, arm-in-arm beneath the umbrella.

'Come on,' said Pierre, wheeling his bicycle and Rosie across the road. Lottie followed.

'I'll leave the bicycle here,' said Pierre, propping it up against the wall. He lifted Rosie out of the basket and handed her to Lottie. 'The corgi's going to have to walk now.' He smiled.

Lottie set Rosie down and attached the lead to her collar. They walked through the gate and along a wide cobbled path lined with tombs. The path sloped gently uphill, and Madeleine and Tom were clearly visible ahead of them. Lottie was careful to keep her distance.

'How big is this place?' she said.

'Enormous. You could spend a whole day walking around it.'

The cemetery felt quiet after the exhilaration of the bicycle ride, all Lottie could hear was the gentle patter of rain. Trees grew among the headstones and monuments which stretched as far as the eye could see. Some tombs were large enough to resemble miniature chapels with arched iron doorways and carved stone decoration. Elsewhere, ivy crept across stone crosses, urns and bronze statues with streaks of oxidised green. Weeping angels and other mournful figures bowed their heads.

'It's almost like a little town,' said Lottie. 'A necropolis.'

'A what?'

'City of the dead. That's what necropolis means.'

'How do you know that?'

'I read it in a book once.'

Pierre gave a shudder. 'It's not the sort of city I want to spend much time in.'

'Do you know your way around?'

'No, I came here once when I was young. I've got a great uncle buried here, that's how I know it's a large cemetery.'

'Where's he buried?'

'I can't remember. I've just noticed something.'

'What?'

'There's hardly anyone around, is there?'

Lottie glanced about. It was empty apart from the distant figures of Madeleine and Tom. 'You're right,' she said. 'It feels quite eerie. Why did they come here?'

'Because it's very romantic to walk in a cemetery.'

'Is it?'

'I don't know!' He laughed. 'I was joking.'

Madeleine and Tom took the left fork in the path and Lottie, Rosie and Pierre followed at a distance. Lottie felt uneasy. A movement in the corner of her eye made her catch her breath, then she saw it was a squirrel scampering across a lichen-covered tomb. She tightened her grip on Rosie's lead, not wanting her to chase off after it. 'Let's hope we don't see a cat,' she said.

'Why?'

'Rosie barks at cats. And if she barks, then Madeleine and Tom will turn round and see us.'

'There's a risk they could do that anyway. If they do, we could just tell them it's a coincidence we're here.'

'Do you think they'd believe that?'

'Probably not.'

'I really don't want to be caught out again.'

'You should have thought about that before you decided to follow Madeleine Lenoir!'

'I realise that. It was only because she'd lied to me about going for a walk. And now I know why, it was because she'd arranged to meet Tom Springer. The fact she's keeping it a secret suggests everyone's supposed to think it's over between them. Perhaps he's not going back to America at all and he's just moved to a different part of Paris in the hope Mrs Lenoir won't find out?'

'Maybe. They must be very much in love.'

'I don't understand why she would fall in love with him.'

'What's wrong with him?'

'He's got a funny wide mouth.'

Pierre laughed. 'He can't help that!'

'I suppose not. Anyway, perhaps we should go back now? We've found out why Madeleine came here and there's probably not much more to see. I'm worried she'll discover us here.'

'Alright then.'

They turned around, and Lottie felt a prickle on the back of her neck. The silence of the cemetery unnerved her. She wanted to be back with the noise and bustle of the streets again.

At that second, a deafening bang split the air. Lottie's heart leapt into her mouth and she dropped to her knees on the cobbles. The echo rang around the cemetery, bouncing off the tombs and headstones. Rosie slipped her lead and scarpered away off the path. Pierre crouched close by. Lottie wanted to follow Rosie, but she was too scared to move. She held her breath.

A second bang sounded.

'Gunshots!' cried Lottie, diving off the path in the same direction as Rosie.

'Lottie!' shouted Pierre.

But she was too scared to respond. She stumbled between the wet tombs and headstones in a blind panic, twisting her ankle on the uneven ground.

Where was Rosie?

She clambered on, then tripped and held out a hand to steady herself, grazing it on the rough stone of a tomb. She kept her head bowed, fearing another shot would soon come.

Up ahead, she saw a flash of brown and white.

'Rosie!'

The corgi skipped behind a headstone. Lottie caught up with her and found her cowering there in the long damp grass. 'Oh Rosie! It's alright. There won't be any more noises. Come on, let me take you back to the hotel.' She picked her up and felt her quivering with fright. The dog pushed her nose under Lottie's chin as she tried to find her way back to a path.

'I'm so sorry,' she said. 'I shouldn't have brought you here.'

Eventually she found a path, but there was no sign of anyone else about. Was it possible someone had fired the gun at her and Pierre? Had it been Madeleine and Tom?

She walked briskly, cuddling Rosie close to her chest. She wanted to get out of the cemetery as quickly as possible.

Running footsteps behind her made her spin round.

She was relieved to see Pierre, looking even redder than before. 'Are you alright?' he asked.

'I think so. You?'

'Not really. Did you see anyone?'

'No.'

'Those were gunshots, weren't they?' said Pierre. 'Were they fired at us?'

'I hope not! We should tell the police.'

'But then we'd have to explain why we were here and tell them we were following Madeleine Lenoir.'

Lottie thought about this. It wasn't the sort of thing she wanted to admit to. 'Let's think about it then.'

'Yes let's do that. And get out of here.'

Chapter Twenty-Six

WHO HAD FIRED the gun at them? Lottie pondered this as she sipped her vegetable soup in *Chez Florent* that evening. Had Tom Springer fired it? Or even Madeleine Lenoir? She and Pierre hadn't mentioned it to the police yet, and she wasn't sure that she wanted to.

'Are you alright, Lottie?' said Mrs Moore. 'You're rather quiet and you keep frowning.'

'I'm fine, just a little bit tired.'

'I'm not surprised. You took another long walk with Rosie this afternoon and you looked exhausted when you got back. You shouldn't let yourself get soaking wet like that, you'll come down with influenza if you're not careful. And then we'll have to postpone our travelling plans!'

'I got a bit carried away.' Lottie forced a smile. She couldn't possibly tell Mrs Moore that someone had fired a gun at her. 'Paris is such an interesting place that I walked on much further than I'd intended. In fact, I even got as far as Tour Saint-Jacques.'

'A what?'

'It's a tall church tower on the Rue de Rivoli. It was once

143

part of a church which was destroyed in the Revolution. It's quite a long way from the hotel but I saw it up ahead and couldn't resist walking to it.'

'Interesting.'

Laughter broke out at Prince Manfred's table, and Mrs Moore's attention was diverted. Lottie felt guilty about fibbing to her employer, but if she'd told her that Madeleine Lenoir had met with Tom Springer, she felt sure Mrs Moore would tell Harriet Lenoir. If that happened, then Lottie could be forced to admit that she'd followed Madeleine Lenoir. Perhaps Madeleine knew she'd followed her? Maybe she'd fired the gun at her? Lottie certainly couldn't tell Mrs Moore about the gunshots, she'd never let her out of her sight again. She hoped she could tell her everything once the case was resolved. But would it ever be resolved?

'Ich heisse Roberta Moore,' said Mrs Moore. 'Und ich bin Amerikaner. What do you think? Does it sound good?'

'Very good.'

'I am called Roberta Moore and I am American. Did you guess it?'

'A little.'

'Soon I'll know more German than you know French. Well, not soon, actually. More like in thirty years' time! It's harder to remember things as you get older. If I'd learned all these German words when I was a girl, then I'd be completely fluent by now.' She gazed longingly at Prince Manfred's table. 'The very best way to learn a language, though, is to practise it.' The prince was chatting animatedly with his friends. He was difficult to miss in his jade green jacket striped with gold and a tangerine silk cravat with a sparkling jewel pinned to it.

Lottie's thoughts turned to Tom Springer. He was more likely to have fired the gun than Madeleine. He could also be the murderer of Jacques Marchand and Lucien Boucher. The more she considered it, the more convinced she became.

But why hadn't he travelled back to America? If he was the murderer, then he would easily escape justice by sailing off across the Atlantic. For some reason, he was still in Paris. Was it his love for Madeleine which kept him here?

'You're deep in thought, Lottie,' said Mrs Moore. 'I hope you're not puzzling over those two terrible murders. There's absolutely nothing we can do about them, you know. You told the police about the argument between Charles Lenoir and Lucien Boucher and you must leave them to it now.'

Two bowls loaded high with profiteroles were brought to their table. 'With the compliments of Prince Manfred,' said the waiter.

'Oh how delightful!' Mrs Moore turned to the prince's table and gave him a grateful wave. 'Danke schön!' she said. He responded with a wave and a grin.

'I said "thank you" to him, Lottie,' said Mrs Moore. 'That was another phrase I learned this afternoon. I'm so pleased I remembered it! I shall get this eaten and then I'm going to thank Prince Manfred in person for this lovely dessert. I'll not let him get away this time!'

Lottie enjoyed the first profiterole with its rich cream and chocolate. She wasn't sure how she'd be able to get through the entire bowlful though.

'What shall we do tomorrow?' said Mrs Moore. 'I'd like to see more of the sights. We haven't even explored the left bank yet, have we?'

'I want to go up the Eiffel Tower.'

'Oh, you and that tower. You're quite insistent on it aren't you?'

There was a sudden movement from the table next to them and Prince Manfred and his party stood up.

'No!' mumbled Mrs Moore, her mouth filled with profiterole. But before she could say anything further, Prince Manfred had left the restaurant again.

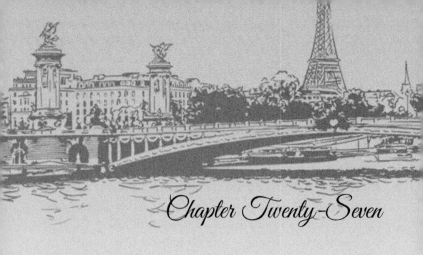

Chapter Twenty-Seven

THE RECEPTIONIST HANDED Lottie an envelope when they returned to the hotel.

'Who's that from?' asked Mrs Moore.

Lottie opened it and pulled out the short note:

Please meet me at Le Canard Rouge, Rue Rouget de Lisle, at your earliest convenience, Madeleine.

A chill stirred in Lottie's stomach. Madeleine could have been the person who'd fired the shots in the graveyard. Could she be planning to shoot at her again?

Lottie told herself it would be impossible. She recalled standing outside *Le Canard Rouge* earlier, it was a bar which would probably be busy at this time of night. She couldn't believe that Madeleine would attempt such a thing. In fact, Lottie felt sure the person who'd fired the shots was far more likely to have been Tom Springer. Did Madeleine wish to meet to apologise? Lottie couldn't imagine that either, it was more likely that she was angry at Lottie for having followed her.

The time at which the note had been written was noted in the top right-hand corner: 9.50 pm. The clock on the wall behind the reception desk showed it was now half-past ten.

'Why does she want you to meet her at this late hour?' said Mrs Moore. 'Can't it wait until the morning? And where is that place? It could be on the other side of Paris for all we know.'

'It's the street where they live,' said Lottie. 'I remember seeing the bar, it's close to their apartment.' There was little doubt that Madeleine was going to confront her. What explanation could Lottie possibly give for following her? She could ignore the note and not go. But she would have to face Madeleine at some point. If she met her this evening, then hopefully matters would be sorted sooner rather than later. And she wouldn't miss a night's sleep worrying about it.

'I'll go and see what she wants.'

'Really? It's ever so late.'

'It might be urgent.'

'If it's that urgent, she could have waited here in the hotel. Why a bar?'

'It's only around the corner from here.'

'Well, I'm going to go up to my room and I'll take Rosie with me. If you insist on going, Lottie, then let's see if the hotel can spare one of its employees to walk you there. I don't like the thought of you alone out there in the dark.'

A BOY from the hotel kitchen was found to walk with Lottie to the meeting place. He strode on ahead of her, seemingly keen to complete the chore. Lottie followed behind, her feet dragging with reluctance. Madeleine couldn't possibly harm her, could she? And then Lottie stopped for a moment, immediately wary of going any further. The thought had just occurred to her that Tom Springer could be there. She couldn't imagine Madeleine trying to harm her, but maybe Tom could. The kitchen boy turned around, as if wondering what she was doing. She felt foolish and continued walking. If he hadn't been accompanying her, she would have turned around and gone back to the hotel.

Lottie had to come up with an explanation for why she'd followed Madeleine. Perhaps it would be alright to tell her she'd become concerned because she saw her getting into a taxi when she'd told her she was going for a walk? Perhaps she could put all the blame onto Pierre because he wasn't here to defend himself? That seemed the easiest tactic but also the most unfair.

The strains of a jazz band drifted from *Le Canard Rouge*, along with excitable chatter and laughter. The hotel kitchen boy opened the door for her, then wished her a good evening before going on his way. Lottie now stood alone in the busy, noisy bar. All the tables were taken and people filled the spaces between them. The men were in shirt sleeves and waistcoats, while the ladies wore colourful flapper dresses with sparkling beads and sequins. The air was stifling and laden with cigarette smoke. White-aproned waiters navigated the throng with expertly balanced trays of drinks and Lottie wondered how she was going to find Madeleine in this crowd.

She threaded her way through the bar, growing dizzy with the effort of checking every face she could see. Her route took her in front of the band and the blast of the trumpet deafened her while the thud of the drums shook her from head to toe.

There was still no sign of Madeleine. Could she be playing a trick on her?

Cool air wafted in through an open door at the back of the bar, Lottie stepped through it to find a walled courtyard where vines crept across a trellis roof and candles flickered on the tables. It was quieter out here, and Lottie immediately felt relieved by the fresher air.

'Lottie.' She turned at the sound of a man's voice. And then she saw Charles Lenoir, cigarette in hand, sitting at a table for two. He gestured at the seat opposite him.

She sat down. 'Hello Charles, have you seen Madeleine?'

'No I haven't.'

'That's strange, she asked me to meet her here.' She hoped Madeleine hadn't been wanting to keep the arrangement a secret.

'She left you a note.'

'Yes. How did you—'

'That wasn't Madeleine,' he said. 'It was me.'

Lottie's chest tightened. Why had he lied? All her preparation for what to say to Madeleine wasn't needed now.

'You wrote the note?'

'Yes. I thought you'd be more likely to come if it had been written by Madeleine.'

There was something stern and cold about his manner, and Lottie didn't like it at all.

'How can I help, Charles?'

'You can help by not talking to the police about me.'

'How do you know about that?'

'Because they told me that someone had heard the conversation between myself and Lucien. I know it was you because I saw you running away after your dog barked!'

'I wasn't prying, if that's what you think it was.'

He gave a snort of disdain.

'When I heard Lucien Boucher had been murdered, I thought they should know about the conversation.'

'Why? And what were you doing listening at that window in the first place? It was a private conversation.'

'I'm sorry I didn't go there intending to listen in on any conversation.'

'Why were you even there?'

'Rosie ran into the courtyard and I had to retrieve her. I recognised your and Lucien's voices when I walked past the window.'

'But you didn't know for sure that it could have been us.'

'No I didn't. But I'm guessing that, because you've summoned me here, it was you.'

He sat back in his chair and sucked on his cigarette.

'You're right, it was. And now, thanks to you, the police consider me a suspect in the murder of Lucien Boucher.'

'Really? But when I spoke to Commissaire Gauthier about it, he didn't even seem that interested. It was a mistake to speak to him.' *But was it really a mistake?* Lottie wondered. *It wasn't, if Charles turned out to be the murderer.* 'I'm sorry,' she added, unsure whether she actually was.

'You need to think more carefully before supposedly helping. Have you got any idea what my family has been going through over the past few days?'

'I've got a reasonably good idea. It must be very difficult and I'm sorry.'

'You can keep apologising all you like, but it's not going to change anything. The police think I'm lying to them. Don't you think my poor mother has been through enough?'

'She has, it's been a difficult time for her. I was only trying to be helpful and maybe I have been. Perhaps the information I've given the police could help catch the murderer?'

'What do you mean by that?' He jutted his jaw.

Lottie took in a breath and decided to be brave. Her voice wavered a little as she spoke. 'I mean that... if you are the murderer, then I've given the police some valuable information, haven't I?'

He leaned forward. 'Do you honestly think I murdered two people?'

'No I don't Charles, you seem quite pleasant and I do feel an awful lot of sympathy for your family. And if the police do their job properly and you've got nothing to hide, then you've got nothing to worry about, I'm sure.'

He sat back again. 'The police can jump to the wrong conclusions and it doesn't help when they're being fed unreliable information from you. The commissaire could only relate some of the conversation to me, which suggests you didn't hear much of it at all. You do realise we were talking about a broken light?'

'Were you?' The conversation had sounded quite serious for such a simple topic.

'Yes, so there you go, you see. You had no idea what we were talking about. You have to keep your nose out of my family's business, Miss Sprigg. You can't just go charging about thinking you can help solve this, it's a complicated case and there are things going on that you know nothing about. So you need to stop thinking of yourself as some sort of detective. You can only be helpful when you're in full possession of the facts. And I can tell you now that you're not.'

'I only did what I thought was right. I'm sorry it's inconvenienced you and I'm sorry to upset you and your family even further. The truth will come out in the end. I feel confident of that.'

'Yes it will, no thanks to you. Does your employer know what you're up to?'

'I'm not up to anything.'

'Yes you are!' he snarled. 'You're snooping! And you've got no right to. I've a good mind to tell Mrs Moore about the trouble you're causing. It would be a shame if you lost your job, wouldn't it? You wouldn't be able to travel and stay in luxury hotels. Where would you be then? Back in Britain working as a maid. That's if you're lucky. Many people take a dim view of someone who's been dismissed from their job.'

Lottie glared at him and felt a bitter taste in her mouth.

'Now keep out of it,' he said. 'And if Maddy has any sense, she'll keep her distance from you too. I shall warn her about you, Lottie, because I think you're trouble.'

'Is something wrong with your breakfast, Lottie?' asked Mrs Moore the following morning. 'You're taking your time over that egg.'

'No, nothing's wrong with it.'

'Are you tired?'

'A little bit.'

'What did Madeleine want?'

'She was, erm... feeling a little bit sad about something, but she didn't tell me what.'

'She asked to meet you but didn't tell you why?'

'I think she wanted some company.'

'Doesn't she have her own friends?'

'I think so, I don't know.'

'Well, we know why she's feeling sad, don't we? That boyfriend of hers has gone back to America.' Mrs Moore took a sip of tea. 'Harriet did well to find out about that liaison.'

Lottie kept mulling over the conversation with Charles. Although she felt she'd done the right thing by telling the police about his conversation with Lucien Boucher, she could also see how much it had upset him. But why? Was it because he didn't like people talking about him to the police? Or did he actually have something to hide?

Mrs Moore got up and retrieved a newspaper which had been left on the neighbouring table. She handed it to Lottie. 'Would you mind having a quick look through and seeing if there's any update on the murder investigations? You'd have thought some progress would have been made by now.'

The headline on the front page concerned the gunshots in Père Lachaise cemetery. No one had been injured, but the identity of the gunman remained a mystery. Police had been called to the cemetery after residents living nearby had heard the shots, but nothing had been found other than two empty bullet casings near the tomb of the playwright Molière.

Lottie felt her heart thud as she read the article. Should she tell the police what she'd seen and heard? She thought better of it for now, wary of Charles's warning the previous evening.

'Anything?' asked Mrs Moore.

Lottie turned the page and found an article which revealed nothing new about either Jacques Marchand's death or Lucien Boucher's. It was intriguing, however, that the supposed intruder hadn't been seen anywhere.

'There's nothing new to report,' said Lottie.

'They are being slow, aren't they? Let's visit Harriet this morning and see how she's faring.'

'Must I go too?' Lottie felt fearful of encountering Charles Lenoir. After telling her to stay away, how was he going to feel if he saw her in his home?

'Of course you must come too. You seem reluctant, though.'

'No, I just wondered if I was needed.'

'I don't blame you for feeling reluctant. This isn't exactly the fun time we had planned in Paris, is it? Two people murdered and the killer still on the loose. I feel rather sorry for

Harriet though, she doesn't seem to have many people to confide in.'

EDMOND AND ROSIE were delighted to see each other. The two dogs skipped off together along the corridor as soon as Lottie and Mrs Moore stepped into the apartment.

'A Parisian love story,' said Mrs Moore, smiling fondly at the dogs.

'I suppose it's something to be happy about,' said Harriet Lenoir, managing a smile. 'Animals always cheer us up, don't they?'

No sooner had she greeted them than Madeleine Lenoir appeared and took Lottie by the arm. 'I've got some new detective books to show you, Lottie, come and see!'

Before she could protest, Lottie was led away by the arm to a little floral sitting room at the front of the apartment. As soon as they were in the room, Madeleine closed the door and Lottie desperately tried to recall the preparations she'd made for their conversation.

Her mind felt empty. She didn't know what to say.

Madeleine's eyes were wide and restless as she leaned back against the door. Lottie retreated to a small chair and hoped this would be over quickly.

'I'm completely shaken up and I have to tell someone about it!' said Madeleine. 'I hope you don't mind me grabbing you like this. I've been having to hide so much and it's awful.' She wiped her hands over her face and began to pace the room. 'I have a confession to make, I told you yesterday afternoon that I was going for a walk but actually I went to see Tom. I wasn't supposed to, he isn't even supposed to be in Paris. My mother somehow found out about our friendship and told him to leave and go back to America! Can you believe it?'

Lottie shook her head, pretending to disbelieve. Every

muscle in her body felt tense as she waited for Madeleine to challenge her.

'It sounds rather mean of Mother, but I think she's worried about what might happen to me if people discover my friendship with Tom. But people needn't know! I just couldn't help myself yesterday. He's moved to an apartment near Père Lachaise cemetery and I'm afraid I went there to meet him. I'm not proud of myself but I care about him so much! You won't tell anyone, will you?'

'No.'

'And you won't believe what happened while we were in the cemetery.'

'What?'

'Someone tried to shoot us!'

'Really? Why would someone do that?'

'I don't know! First Jacques was murdered and then Lucien Boucher. And then someone tried to shoot me!'

'That's awful! How frightening for you? Have you told your mother?'

'No, that's just the problem, you see! I can't! She doesn't know I was there. No one does!'

Lottie felt a little relieved that Madeleine hadn't noticed her in the cemetery. She was also relieved that the shots hadn't been fired by Madeleine or Tom. So who had fired them?

'Perhaps the shots weren't aimed at you Maddy, perhaps they were firing at someone else?'

'Such as who?'

'I don't know. Did you see the person with the gun?'

'No! The shots came out of nowhere!'

'What a mystery. I saw a report about it in the newspaper this morning.'

'It's in the newspaper? What did it say?'

'Not much. Only that the shots were heard, but the gunman wasn't seen.'

'That's exactly what happened!' Madeleine flopped into a chair.

'So the gunman could have been firing at you, Tom, or someone else. Or even a pigeon.'

'No! Why would someone want to hurt a pigeon?'

'I don't know.' Lottie felt as puzzled by the episode as Madeleine was.

'You really don't realise how loud a gun is until you hear one go off,' said Madeleine. 'It's so loud! Especially in a quiet place like a cemetery. I've never known a week like this one. I wish I could wind time back to a fortnight ago when everything was normal. I just don't know what to do about it.'

'Maybe you could tell the police about the gunshots?'

'I can't! Because then my mother would find out.'

'She might not.'

'My mother finds out everything.'

'Would it be really so bad if she knew?'

'Yes! Probably! Oh, I don't know! And to make matters worse, Lottie, Tom is acting strange.'

'In what way?'

'I don't know. But I think he has a secret and he won't tell me what it is.'

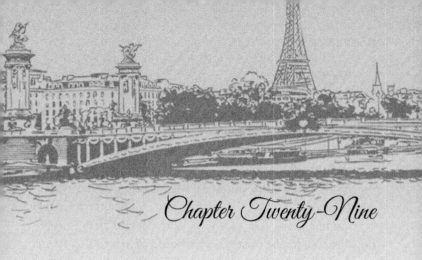

Chapter Twenty-Nine

AFTER LUNCH, Mrs Moore retired to her room to learn some more German. Lottie took Rosie out for a walk and loitered near the bakery in the hope she'd see Pierre. It wasn't long before he arrived on his bicycle.

'Are you waiting for me?' he asked with a grin.

'No.' She felt her face heat up. 'I was just passing.'

'That's a shame. I hoped you'd be waiting.'

'I saw Madeleine Lenoir this morning,' she said, purposefully changing the topic, so she didn't become even more bashful. 'And she told me that someone shot at her and Tom Springer in Père Lachaise cemetery. They didn't see the gunman, they just heard the shots. Like we did.'

'So neither she or Tom fired the gun?'

'It seems not.'

'Do you think she's telling the truth?'

'Yes, I do.'

'Well, I feel a bit better now, I was worrying that they'd tried to shoot us,' said Pierre. 'But who was it? I was awake thinking about it last night and I decided it was Tom Springer.'

'Why?'

'It's obvious why he wanted Jacques Marchand dead. And I think he bribed Lucien Boucher so he could get in and out of the building without supposedly being seen. Then, maybe Lucien Boucher felt bad about what he'd done and decided he was going to tell the police.'

'How would Tom know he was planning to do that?' asked Lottie.

'I don't know. Or maybe he just decided that Lucien Boucher couldn't be trusted, so he murdered him too.'

'But if Tom's the murderer, then I don't understand why he remains in Paris.'

'He's in love with Madeleine,' said Pierre.

'But she told me earlier that she suspects he's keeping a secret from her.'

'The secret could be that he's the murderer!'

'I suppose it could.'

'Or maybe Madeleine's the murderer?' said Pierre.

'She could have murdered Jacques Marchand. But Lucien Boucher?'

'I can't work out yet what her motive would be for murdering him.

'There's Charles Lenoir too,' said Lottie. "I think he's the most likely culprit.'

'Why?'

Lottie told him about the meeting with Charles the previous evening.

'I've a good mind to have a word with him!' said Pierre, scowling.

'Please don't, it won't help anything.'

'But you don't deserve to be spoken to in that way!'

'It makes sense if he's the murderer, Pierre. And if he is, I'm sure he could get a lot nastier.'

HARRIET LENOIR STOOD on a balcony overlooking the courtyard. She clasped the locket which hung around her neck, it contained a lock of her beloved late husband's hair. 'I'm sorry, Antoine, that it's come to this.' She gave a sniff. 'But if you hadn't gone and died, then I wouldn't have had to set Maddy up with that dreadful Marchand family. I never liked Jacques, what a dull, ignorant young man he was. But Maddy didn't seem to mind him too much and the marriage would have put an end to all our problems. I've done my best to secure a good future for this family, but all my efforts appear to have been in vain. If only Maddy didn't have a mind of her own! She's always been strong-willed, just like you, Antoine. I can only hope that I can secure another good marriage for her. But if the Marchands found out she was unfaithful to their son, then I know I shall be held partly accountable! Our reputation will be in tatters! All I can hope is that the police arrest someone shortly and we can all—'

'Mother!'

'Oh, what now?'

Harriet left the balcony and returned to the room to find Madeleine there, red-faced and snivelling.

'What's happened?'

'Oh, everything!'

Sit down, Madeleine, and tell me what the problem is.

'Oh Mother! I have so much to tell you. I can't hide it any longer!'

Chapter Thirty

'EVERYTHING IS GETTING COMPLETELY out of hand,' said Harriet Lenoir. She had unexpectedly called on Mrs Moore and they now sat in the hotel restaurant for afternoon tea. The table was overladen with sandwiches and cakes.

'Madeleine has just given me a long, tearful confession,' continued Mrs Lenoir. 'And it turns out that dreadful artist hasn't left for America after all! I asked her what he'd done with my money and she didn't know I'd given him any money, so now she's even more angry and upset than she was before.'

'He's not left yet?' said Mrs Moore.

'No! And I don't think he has any intention of doing so!'

'Good golly.'

'She's also told me she suspects he's hiding a secret. And the more she tries to find out what it is, the more he won't tell her. And I'll tell you something worse.'

'Oh no, what can be worse?'

'Someone tried to shoot her in a cemetery?'

'What?'

Lottie listened to the familiar tale as she pulled off a piece of ham sandwich and passed it to Rosie under the table.

'I can scarcely believe it,' said Mrs Moore, once her friend had finished. 'Whatever next?'

'I think it's quite obvious that her boyfriend is the murderer and I shall be telling the police so.'

'You think he did it?'

'Yes. He wanted her all to himself, which is why he murdered Jacques and, as for Lucien Boucher... well I don't know, they must have had a falling out about something.'

'Maybe he bribed Lucien Boucher to allow him in and out of the building on the evening of the murder,' said Lottie. 'And then he grew worried Lucien would tell, so he murdered him.'

'Yes!' Harriet Lenoir pointed at Lottie. 'That has to be it! There can be no other explanation, can there?' She took a sip of tea. 'I think we've cracked it. And to think that, all along, that awful artist has been manipulating my daughter! She would never have behaved like that before she met him, it's all his fault. As soon as we've finished here, I shall go back to my apartment and telephone the police. Would you mind accompanying me, Roberta? It's just that it can be so wearisome trying to do everything on my own.'

'Of course, Harriet.'

LOTTIE HAD AN HOUR TO HERSELF. She hadn't forgotten about the tiny scraps of paper she'd picked up from the lobby floor. She walked over to the reception desk.

'Can you tell me where Rue Legouvé is, please?' she asked the receptionist.

'I don't know it, I'm afraid.'

Lottie felt her shoulders slump. She knew there was a chance that the street wasn't even in Paris.

'I shall have a look at a map,' added the receptionist. He

bent down behind his desk for a while and then reappeared with a map, which he opened out across the polished desktop. He read down a list of street names then peered closely at the map.

'Ah ha! Rue Legouvé is here in the 10th arrondissement.' He poked at it with the end of his pen.

'What's the easiest way to get there?'

'Ask the footman to hail you a taxi.'

'I don't have the money for a taxi.'

'Don't you? Ah, then you must take the tram. Take the number twenty-four to Place de la République and you can walk from there.'

LOTTIE FELT a sense of accomplishment when she found the tram with number twenty-four on the front. She sat on a wooden seat alongside the other passengers with Rosie on her lap. At Place de la République, she had to ask a few people for directions, her route took her alongside a canal before she eventually found the street she was looking for.

It was a quiet, unremarkable road, narrow and lined with small apartment blocks. A scruffy black cat crossed the street and Rosie barked at it.

The little scrap of paper had a number eight on it. Lottie soon found the corresponding building and felt a little disappointed. It was a small single door with brown, peeling paint.

How had the address of this place found its way onto the floor of the lobby in the Lenoir family's apartment block? Lottie thought about knocking at the door, but didn't know who to ask for. Then she was struck by the thought she'd come here in error. The address probably had nothing to do with the Lenoir family, Lucien Boucher, or anyone in that building. It had just been a torn up and discarded piece of paper. Maybe used by a delivery boy or a postman who'd dropped it when visiting the apartment building.

'I don't know what to do, Rosie,' she said. 'Shall we go back? At least the tram ride was fun.'

She turned to leave when the door opened and an old lady in a headscarf stepped out. Lottie felt the need to explain her presence. 'Do you mind me asking if you live here?'

The old lady narrowed her eyes. 'Who's asking?'

'My name's Lottie Sprigg and I came here because I found this address on a torn-up piece of paper.'

'I don't see what that's got to do with me.' She began to walk off.

'Wait! Have you ever known someone with the surname Lenoir?'

There was no response.

'Lucien Boucher?' called out Lottie.

The old lady stopped, then slowly turned around. 'I think there was a Mr and Mrs Boucher living here a long time ago.'

'How long ago?'

'It could have been thirty years ago. They were a young couple, recently married. They didn't live here long, I think she left him and then he moved away.'

'What did they look like?'

The old lady thought. 'He was tall and untidy looking. I remember he had a distinctive stoop. She was much shorter, she had fair hair and was quite pretty. I spoke to him once or twice but never to her. That's all I can tell you, I hope it helps. Au revoir.'

'Thank you for your help!' Lottie called after her.

So she was standing outside Lucien Boucher's former home. He'd lived here with his wife and Lottie recalled him mentioning he'd moved to Normandy in his twenties after his wife had left him. But why had their former address been

written on a piece of paper? And why had the paper been
ripped up?

'POOR HARRIET,' said Mrs Moore as she and Lottie dined at *Chez Florent* that evening. Prince Manfred and his group had not yet arrived at their table. 'She's reported everything to the police now and urged them to keep the friendship between Madeleine and that artist quiet, but it could all come out, you know. It sounds dreadful of me to say it, but she's brought some of this on herself.'

'How?'

'By trying to force a marriage between Madeleine and someone she didn't want to marry. I realise it's the sort of thing that's been done for centuries, but it doesn't work with modern young women these days, much as we'd like it to. I realise it's been difficult for Harriet, she's a widow and she has to maintain her status. But young women these days have minds of their own. It's quite obvious Madeleine didn't wish to marry Jacques and, by trying to force it, Harriet has just brought more problems upon herself. Had Harriet allowed Madeleine to find a young man of her choice, then I'm sure she would have opted for someone more sensible than that

American artist. Perhaps the match wouldn't have quite offered the status that Harriet was looking for, but then perhaps she was aiming a little too high. The pursuit of blind ambition can result in a great deal of misfortune. And then Madeleine decided to fall in love with a murderer!'

'You think Tom Springer did it?'

'Well, Harriet says he did, and she knows far more about it all than me. I can only agree with her. I'm hoping that the police are arresting Tom Springer as we speak and this whole sorry mess can be resolved. How awful, though, for it to have resulted in two deaths! None of this needed to have happened.'

'It will be interesting to hear Tom Springer's explanation.'

'I've never met the fellow, but he strikes me as the sort to talk his way out of things. The police won't fall for it, I'm sure. Especially that Commissaire Gauthier, he seems like a sensible no-nonsense man.' She glanced at the empty table. 'I wonder where Prince Manfred has got to this evening?'

The waiter arrived to take their order.

'Lottie, please can you ask the waiter what has happened to Prince Manfred?'

Lottie asked him the question.

'I believe he has left Paris,' came the reply.

Lottie translated for Mrs Moore.

'*Left Paris*?' Her mouth hung open. 'Where's he gone?'

The waiter said he would ask the maître d'. A moment later, the important looking maître d' arrived at their table.

'My employer, Mrs Moore, would like to know where Prince Manfred of Bavaria has travelled to,' said Lottie.

'The prince left for Cairo today,' said the maître d'. 'It is a great shame because we have very much enjoyed entertaining his party here every evening. He will visit us again when he is next in Paris.'

'What's he saying?' asked Mrs Moore.

Lottie translated the reply.

'Cairo?' gasped Mrs Moore, clasping her hands to her chest. 'But why is he going all the way to Egypt?'

'Is everything alright?' asked the concerned maître d'.

'Yes,' said Lottie. 'It's a bit of a surprise for my employer.'

Chapter Thirty-Two

AFTER BREAKFAST THE FOLLOWING MORNING, Mrs Moore set about making arrangements for Cairo. She asked the hotel receptionist to book tickets for the Simplon-Orient Express, which would take them from Paris to the port of Trieste in northern Italy. From there, they would sail to Alexandria, then travel by train to Cairo.

'We'll depart tomorrow and it will take us five days to get there,' she told Lottie. 'Isn't that wonderful? Just five days! I've never been to Egypt before, I can't wait.'

Lottie felt a tingle of anticipation. She pictured pyramids, the Sphinx, hot sunshine and busy markets. But she really didn't know what to expect at all. And she didn't want to leave Paris while the murders of Jacques Marchand and Lucien Boucher remained unsolved.

'We'll visit Harriet Lenoir this morning and let her know that we're departing tomorrow,' said Mrs Moore. 'I feel that I'm abandoning her a little, but I can't stay here and lend her a sympathetic ear forever, can I? I have my own needs to pursue.'

'Perhaps we could stay a day or two longer?'

'There's no need Lottie. And besides, I want to meet Prince Manfred in Cairo, if we leave it too long, then he'll be on his travels again. He never seems to stay in one place for too long.'

LOTTIE, Mrs Moore and Rosie made the short walk from the hotel to the Lenoir family's apartment block.

'There's that young delivery boy who likes to make eyes at you,' said Mrs Moore.

'He doesn't make eyes at me!' spluttered Lottie, as heat flushed into her face.

Pierre was wheeling his bicycle towards them. He greeted Lottie with a grin.

'We're leaving for Cairo tomorrow,' she explained.

'Cairo?' His face fell. 'You're leaving?'

'I'm afraid so.'

'Why Cairo?'

'My employer has an acquaintance there who she wishes to see.'

Pierre gave a nod and pursed his lips. 'Enjoy your time there.'

'I'll come and see you before I leave.'

'Will you?'

'Yes, I promise.'

'I will see you around.'

Lottie felt a lump in her throat as she watched him wheel his bicycle away.

'I've no idea what the pair of you were talking about just now, but I have a good idea,' said Mrs Moore. 'The poor boy, he looks broken-hearted.'

'No, he's not, he'll be fine.' Lottie's response was just an attempt to put a brave face on the situation. She hadn't known Pierre long, but she knew she would miss him.

. . .

'ROBERTA! THIS IS A SURPRISE.' Harriet Lenoir welcomed them into her sitting room. Lottie felt a twinge of sadness as she watched Rosie skip off with Edmond. It seemed a shame that the pair would soon be parted.

'So what brings you here?' asked Mrs Lenoir.

'News of our departure I'm afraid, Harriet,' said Mrs Moore.

'No! Are you going back to London?'

'We're off to Cairo.'

'Cairo?'

'I learned last night that Prince Manfred is on his way there.'

'Is he indeed? Well, what a surprise. Perhaps I can come with you?'

'I beg your pardon?'

'Is that not a good idea?'

'I, er... hadn't even considered such a thing. Erm...'

'I've always wanted to go to Cairo. What is there for me here?'

'Your children.'

'They're old enough to lead their own lives now. Antoine's gone and we've had two horrible murders which means I don't feel comfortable living in this apartment anymore. I could sell some things and join you.'

'And what about Madeleine?'

Mrs Lenoir sighed. 'I shall leave her with instructions on how to find a suitable husband, but I fear that my own attempts will only be met with failure again.'

'Not necessarily.'

The excitement which Lottie had felt earlier was dwindling. She didn't want Harriet Lenoir to travel to Cairo with them. She had grown accustomed to having Mrs Moore and Rosie for company, a third person would ruin things.

As the two women talked, Lottie muttered an excuse that she was going to see where Rosie had gone, then sidled out of the room. Out in the corridor, she headed for the main staircase and began to climb it for the first time since Jacques Marchand's murder. She'd gone over numerous encounters and conversations in her mind, and seeing the drawing room again could possibly jog a few more memories.

The drawing room was just as Lottie had remembered, furnished in white and gold and filled with Mrs Lenoir's treasures. Little appeared to have changed in this room since Jacques's murder. As Lottie glanced about, she recalled the conversation that evening about the various ornaments. Mrs Lenoir's favourite gold and porcelain clock still sat on the mantelpiece with the two matching candelabras on either side of it. The pair of Victorian marble lamps which Mrs Lenoir had pointed out were still on the sideboard.

Lottie recalled the lamp which Mrs Moore had liked. It had been the one with the green onyx base and the fringed lampshade and had sat on a table by the fireplace. That lamp was now missing.

On the night of Jacques's murder, Charles had said he'd found him lying by the sideboard. Lottie looked at the spot now. There was nothing there except the polished wooden floor and an oriental rug. A cold tingle ran down Lottie's spine, she gave a shudder and decided she'd seen enough.

She left the room and made her way down the staircase. A cold sensation lingered on the back of her neck. As she made her way back towards the sitting room, she glanced back up at the staircase and startled. At the top stood Charles Lenoir, leaning on his crutches. He stared back at her, his face expressionless.

. . .

'Lottie!' Madeleine greeted her as soon as she stepped into the sitting room, her reception couldn't have been more different to her brother's. 'I've just heard you're leaving us!'

'Yes. We're going to Cairo.'

'Well, I shall miss you. Have you heard the news? Tom was arrested late last night. I've told Mother everything now, I couldn't keep the secrets anymore, they were tearing me up inside. Mother told the police about him.'

'You think he's a murderer?'

'I don't know what to think!' Madeleine's face crumpled. 'I suppose he must be! But I don't think he can be. Oh, I don't know anymore! I knew he was hiding something from me, though, and I suppose it was the fact he'd committed murder. What else could it possibly be?'

Charles appeared in the doorway. 'Commissaire Gauthier is here,' he said. 'Apparently, there are a few things he wishes to discuss with us.'

'Again?' said Mrs Lenoir. 'Why can't he just leave us in peace?'

'It's regarding Tom Springer,' said Charles. 'Do you want me to send him away?'

'I can't imagine him taking kindly to that. Well, if he's got some news on Tom Springer, then let him in, hopefully he'll be quick.'

A few moments later, Commissaire Gauthier stood in the centre of the sitting room, puffing on his pipe. Mrs Moore and Mrs Lenoir sat in the yellow armchairs, while Charles and Madeleine sat on two chairs at a table. There was nowhere to sit for the detective.

'Would you mind bringing in a chair from the study, Lottie?' asked Mrs Lenoir.

Although Lottie agreed with an acquiescent smile, she

hoped Mrs Lenoir wouldn't be accompanying them to Egypt. She was already treating Lottie like a member of her own staff. She found two wooden chairs in the study and brought them into the sitting room. The detective thanked her and positioned his chair in the middle of the room. Lottie put herself by the window.

'I apologise for interrupting your gathering,' said the commissaire. 'I have some news about Tom Springer. Do you wish to excuse your guests before I begin, Mrs Lenoir?'

'Is it something they shouldn't hear?'

'It's probably something they'll find out in due course.'

'Then I'm more than happy for them to stay. Mrs Moore is a good friend of mine.'

'Very well, I'll continue.' He inhaled on his pipe. 'I think we'll get a confession from Mr Springer before long, but he's still denying everything.'

'Well, he would, wouldn't he?' said Mrs Lenoir.

'He's used many excuses to persuade us why he must be released.'

'Oh I'm sure he has!'

'He says he needs to work, he's desperately short of money.'

'Which is why he chose Madeleine in the first place.'

'For money?' said Madeleine, her nostrils flaring. 'He chose me for love!'

Mrs Lenoir said nothing.

'He tells me he needs to urgently work and earn money,' said the detective.

'And?'

'He tells me the money is needed for his newborn daughter.'

Chapter Thirty-Three

THE ROOM WAS SO quiet that Lottie could hear her heartbeat thudding in her ears.

'Why are you all looking at me?' protested Madeleine. 'Tom doesn't have a daughter, it must be a mistake!'

The commissaire cleared his throat. 'Mr Springer is quite adamant he has a daughter. He told me he was notified of the fact by letter a week ago.'

Madeleine's mouth hung open. Lottie felt a little sorry for her.

Mrs Lenoir sighed. 'I suppose this demonstrates the man is just as immoral as I thought he was.'

'Who's the mother?' asked Charles.

'Mr Springer hasn't told us and it's irrelevant to our investigation.'

Madeleine slumped in her chair and covered her face with her hands.

'Well, it's just as well the man is going to be locked away where he can't cause any more trouble,' said Mrs Lenoir. 'The scandal which he could bring to our family is enormous. The news of his illegitimate child must never be discussed outside of these four walls. If only you had never got involved with him, Madeleine! Just think what could happen if anyone learns you've associated with such a man! I think you should come with us to Cairo.'

'Cairo?' wailed Madeleine.

'Yes, we all need to leave Paris for a while and allow the dust to settle. This family needs a fresh start.'

'I'm not going to Cairo!'

'You can't remain in Paris because there's a risk this news will get out. The affair was bad enough, Maddy, but an affair with a man who also has an illegitimate child and has murdered two people? That's ten, no twenty, times worse.'

Madeleine began to sob and Lottie noticed her mother showed no sign of comforting her. Lottie decided that now was the moment to speak up. 'I don't think Tom Springer is a murderer,' she said.

Heads turned to look at her.

'Oh, come on, Lottie,' said Mrs Moore. 'The police have arrested him. Of course he is!'

'Why would he risk a death sentence if he's recently become a father?'

'Fathers are just as capable of committing murder as anyone else,' said Mrs Moore.

Lottie persisted. 'If Tom Springer murdered Jacques Marchand, then how did he get in and out of the building with no one seeing him?'

'It's quite simple,' said Mrs Lenoir. 'He was in allegiance with Lucien Boucher. You even suggested that yourself, Lottie, yesterday.'

'But why did Lucien Boucher allow him into the building?'

'He must have paid him.'

'Tom didn't have any money,' said Madeleine. 'He was always asking me for money.'

'I hope you didn't give him any!' said Mrs Lenoir.

'I gave him a little.'

'Was it enough to bribe the gardien?' asked Lottie.

'I wouldn't have said so,' said Madeleine. 'But I don't know how desperate Lucien Boucher was for money. Perhaps he was easily bought.'

'Miss Sprigg has raised a good question,' said the commissaire. 'We don't know how Tom Springer got in and out of the building without being seen and he won't tell us how he did it.'

'Probably because he didn't murder Jacques,' said Lottie.

'So who did?' asked Charles, folding his arms.

'It has to be someone who was already in the building,' said Lottie.

'Lucien Boucher?' suggested Mrs Moore.

'No, but Mr Boucher was definitely causing trouble for the Lenoir family,' said Lottie.

'In what way?' asked Madeleine. 'I don't remember him causing any trouble.'

'I overheard part of a conversation he had with Charles,' said Lottie.

'Oh, here we go!' he snapped. 'And you're going to tell the police all about it again.'

'You wanted him to leave,' Lottie said. 'And you offered him money, but he refused.'

'Did you Charles?' asked Mrs Lenoir.

'It was just a conversation about a broken light!'

'I heard Lucien Boucher say that a crime had been committed,' said Lottie. 'And that people have to face what they've done in the past.'

'What crime?' asked Mrs Lenoir.

'I've no idea,' said Charles. 'The man was talking nonsense, as usual, and that's why I wanted him to leave. We didn't want someone like him working in our apartment building. I can't understand why he was even recruited.'

'We have discussed the conversation between Mr Lenoir and Mr Boucher,' said the commissaire. 'And it doesn't shed any light on the two murders.'

'Perhaps it does if you combine it with some other information,' said Lottie.

'Such as what?' said Mrs Moore. 'What have you been up to this time?'

'I found some pieces of torn up paper in the lobby,' said Lottie. She turned to the commissaire. 'Did you find some remnants of torn up paper on the floor after Mr Boucher's death?'

'We found a few pieces. But we couldn't work out what they were from.'

'Something important was written on that paper and someone wanted to destroy it,' said Lottie. 'Perhaps it caused the dispute between Mr Boucher and his murderer?'

'Or perhaps it had nothing to do with him at all?' said Charles.

'But it did,' said Lottie. 'I found two fragments. One just had part of a word on it and no meaning, but the other contained part of a Paris address. I visited that address yesterday.'

'You did what, Lottie?' said Mrs Moore. 'You didn't tell me this!'

'It was Rue Legouvé,' said Lottie. 'Does the address mean anything to anyone?' She glanced around at the blank faces.

'What happened when you went there?' asked Mrs Moore.

'I spoke to a lady who lived there, and she told me that Mr Boucher and his wife lived there thirty years ago.'

Charles laughed. 'And why is this relevant?'

'That's exactly what I thought to begin with,' said Lottie. 'Why would an old address for Mr Boucher be written on a piece of paper which was torn up around the same time he was murdered? I decided it must have had some relevance.'

'Or no relevance at all,' said Charles.

'Someone wanted to destroy the information on that piece of paper,' said Lottie. 'And I think that could be the reason he was murdered. Someone wanted him silenced. Is that why you asked him to leave, Charles?'

'No. You're quite mistaken. Now this is enough, you're a... what are you exactly? An assistant to Mrs Moore. Little more than a servant. You've got some gall standing in my home and throwing accusations around.'

'I want to hear what Lottie has to say,' said Madeleine.

'Do you? Well I don't. I think the servant girl fancies herself as some sort of detective and—'

'Charles,' said his mother. 'Don't get carried away with yourself.'

'And why are you defending her, Mother? After all, your reputation has been at stake throughout this.'

'My reputation, you mean,' said Madeleine.

The commissaire cleared his throat. 'Was Mr Boucher silenced, Mr Lenoir?'

'I've no idea!' said Charles.

'He said something about crimes committed long ago,' said Mrs Moore.

'*She* said that,' said Charles, pointing at Lottie. 'She's recounting a conversation she heard through a shuttered window. She can't even prove it was me and Mr Boucher she overheard!'

'You told Lucien Boucher he was causing trouble and should leave,' said Lottie. 'I think this means he knew something. Was he threatening to tell?'

'I don't know!' said Charles.

'Could it have threatened the wedding?' asked Lottie.

'What?' said Mrs Lenoir.

'I don't understand,' said Madeleine.

'Mr Marchand's father is an important man,' said Lottie.

'The marriage of Madeleine and Jacques could have put the Marchand family reputation at stake if the Lenoir family was caught up in scandal. Lucien Boucher had only recently started his job here as a gardien and his appearance was quite sudden, wasn't it? I think he was here to make trouble.'

'That's one thing I'd agree with,' said Charles.

'But what was he making trouble about?' asked Mrs Moore. 'That's what confuses me.'

'His secret,' said Lottie. 'I think he was Mrs Lenoir's first husband.'

Chapter Thirty-Four

MADELEINE GASPED. Lottie noticed Charles showed little reaction.

'Is this true, Harriet?' said Mrs Moore. 'You were once married to Lucien Boucher?'

Harriet Lenoir's eyes were fixed on Lottie. 'A long time ago.'

'Oh,' said Mrs Moore. 'That is a surprise! The man did have some charm, though. Is it such a terrible secret?'

'I never knew about it!' said Madeleine. 'Did you Charles?'

'Only when Mr Boucher told me about it.'

'How did you work this out, Lottie?' asked Mrs Moore.

'I remember Mrs Lenoir telling us she came to Paris at the age of eighteen and that she married Antoine Lenoir when she was twenty-six. So there were eight years before she married him and she didn't really explain what she did during that time.'

'She didn't have to explain it,' said Mrs Moore.

'No, she didn't, but there was something about the way Mrs Lenoir spoke. She paused as if she'd remembered something which she didn't want to tell us. And then there was an uncomfortable silence at dinner.'

'What silence was that?' asked Mrs Moore.

'It was when you mentioned you were unusual in having been married three times because most people only married once. I realise now there was an awkward silence because Mrs Lenoir had also been married more than once. I think Mrs Lenoir married Mr Boucher thirty years ago and they lived at 8 Rue Legouvé.'

'Is that right, Mother?' asked Madeleine.

'Yes,' replied Mrs Lenoir stiffly.

'I must say that, in this day and age, it's not dreadfully uncommon for a lady to have made a misalliance in her youth,' said Mrs Moore. 'This can't be the secret which people lost their lives over, can it?'

'I don't understand what happened with Jacques,' said Madeleine. 'Did he find out you were married to Mr Boucher, Mother?'

'Yes, he did,' said Charles.

'And wait... you murdered him because of it, Charles?' Madeleine's face grew red and twisted. 'I can't believe it! You murdered Jacques Marchand because he found out Mother was married to Lucien Boucher before she married Father?'

Charles said nothing.

'My brother murdered my fiancé!' wailed Madeleine.

Lottie waited for her to calm herself, then prepared herself for the next difficult announcement. 'Mr Boucher said a crime had been committed,' she said. 'I wondered what crime it could possibly be. Then I recalled something which Mr Boucher told me and Mrs Moore. He told us he and his wife had never divorced. I think the crime he discussed with Charles was bigamy.'

'What?' Mrs Moore cried out. 'Lottie! Are you really accusing my friend of such a thing?'

MARTHA BOND

'It seems she is,' said Harriet Lenoir, continuing to give Lottie an icy stare.

'Bigamy! No! Why Mother?' cried Madeleine. 'If Jacques knew you had done such a thing, then he would have asked his family to call the wedding off!'

'And that's exactly what he was going to do,' said Mrs Lenoir calmly. 'He spoke to me before dinner the other evening and told me that Lucien Boucher had told him he was my husband. He said he would tell his parents about it and that he couldn't go through with the marriage and risk damaging the reputation of his father's electoral campaign.'

'Oh, Harriet!' said Mrs Moore. 'How awful! Why would Lucien Boucher turn up and do such a thing?'

'It seems he never forgave me for leaving him.'

'How did he find you?'

'He discovered I'd married again when he saw an announcement in the newspaper. And Antoine was reasonably well known, so I suppose it wasn't difficult to find out where we lived. Perhaps he spied on us over the years? I don't like to think that, but it's possible.' She gave a shudder. 'Anyway, he never made trouble for me while Antoine was around, presumably he was too cowardly for that. But once I became a widow, he considered me as fair game.'

'So that's why he left it all these years,' said Mrs Moore. 'He bore a grudge for a very long time indeed.'

'And he got a job here as the gardien!' said Madeleine. 'Why do that?'

'He told me it was because he wanted me to see him every day and be reminded of what I'd done,' said Mrs Lenoir. 'He said if I tried to get him dismissed, then he'd reveal our secret. He was an extremely bitter man. He was jealous of the life I'd made for myself and he wanted to ruin it.'

'So he got the job of gardien here just to do that?' said Mrs Moore.

'Yes. His mind was twisted, wasn't it? I did wonder why the previous gardien, Mr Fornier, left so suddenly. And when Lucien appeared in his place, I got the shock of my life. Lucien must have forced him to leave, I don't know how, exactly. Perhaps he threatened him.'

'Why didn't you just divorce Lucien?' asked Madeleine.

'Because I didn't have the means to do so, I was young and foolish and had made a mistake. I'd only recently arrived in Paris and I fell for his charms. I was swept away by him just like you were swept away by that rogue Tom Springer. These men know how to make you feel like the most important lady in the world, but they're unreliable and worthless. We married in secret because my parents wouldn't have approved. And I realised within a matter of months that I had made a mistake. And it was almost impossible to undo! What a horrible feeling it was. After I left him, I pretended I'd never been married at all. After all, who was going to find out? If your father had known I was already married, he wouldn't have been interested in me.'

'He would!' said Madeleine. 'And you could have told him. He could have paid for your divorce!'

'He would never have married a divorcee! This was nearly thirty years ago. His family, like many, was very traditional and it would have been unthinkable.'

'So you married Father, and he had no idea you were already married,' said Madeleine.

'Yes. I'm not proud of myself. I never wished to deceive your father, he was the man I truly loved, and it's been terribly difficult ever since he left us. But lying about a previous marriage is probably more common than you realise. I couldn't have known that the dreadful man would turn up on my doorstep all these years later. I can't tell you what a state I was in when I saw him here. After all those years! He'd failed to make any sort of decent life of his own.'

'What did he want from you?' asked Mrs Moore.

'Revenge. He told me I'd destroyed him, so he was going to do the same to me. And that began with him telling Charles I was a bigamist. Then he told Jacques and ruined my daughter's wedding hopes. I couldn't allow him to tell anyone else.'

'So you asked Charles to murder the pair of them!' said Madeleine. 'How awful! I realise Lucien was a horrid man, but that doesn't justify murder. And you ruined my wedding!'

'It was already ruined!'

'But you made everything even worse! What an evil pair you and Charles are!'

Lottie took in a breath, then made her next announcement. 'I don't think Charles was the murderer.'

'He wasn't?' said Madeleine.

'I visited the drawing room earlier,' said Lottie. 'And I noticed there was a lamp missing. Presumably it was the lamp which was used to hit Jacques Marchand, it had a green onyx base and a fringed lampshade.'

The commissaire nodded. 'That was the lamp which was used as a weapon.'

'Jacques Marchand was found lying on the floor by the sideboard,' said Lottie. 'And on the sideboard were two more lamps, both with marble bases. You'd have thought the murderer would have grabbed the nearest lamp to hit Jacques Marchand with. Instead, they went across the room to grab the lamp from the table by the fireplace. The murderer didn't want to use one of the valuable lamps as a weapon. Who else would have cared about the value of the lamp other than Mrs Lenoir?'

There was silence as everyone thought about this.

Lottie continued, 'I even remember Mrs Lenoir telling us she was relieved the murderer had chosen the least valuable lamp in the room.'

'It doesn't mean anything,' snapped Charles. 'Jacques

could have been hit with the lamp by the fireplace, then crawled over to the sideboard.'

The commissaire puffed on his pipe and stared at Mrs Lenoir, as if awaiting her response. Lottie clenched her jaw, anxious to see what her reaction would be.

Eventually Mrs Lenoir spoke. 'Well Roberta, I certainly regret the day I bumped into you and your assistant in Jardin des Tuileries. How I wish I had never extended a hand of friendship!'

'Please tell me you're not a murderer, Harriet! Surely Lottie has got it all wrong?'

'She's quite clever, isn't she? Although I wish she'd got it all wrong, too.'

'You murdered Jacques!' said Madeleine.

'Yes, I did! And you should have seen the smug manner in which he addressed me the other evening before dinner. He looked at me as though I wasn't fit to lick his boots! And you should have heard him, Maddy. And what was more, he was going to tell his parents about it. Everyone would have known! And if they had, then you would never have married well, Maddy. So in that fleeting moment, I had to accept that the marriage wouldn't happen. But was I going to accept that my reputation was ruined and that you would struggle to find a new husband? No, I would not! I couldn't bear standing there listening to the silly little fool lecturing me about my morals. What did he know about anything? I had to think quickly. He'd spoken to me before the dinner and I didn't want him returning to his parents that evening and telling them the news.

'Our search for Edmond that evening provided the perfect distraction. I followed Jacques to the drawing room and then I grabbed the lamp. And yes, it was the cheapest one which I cared little for! I knew I could pretend an intruder had done the job, and I pulled out the drawers and took some silver to convince everyone. But it seems young Lottie here was too clever for that. And as for Lucien Boucher, he'd ruined my family's future, and he was going to ruin much more! I visited him in his apartment and he showed me a letter he was going to send to a newspaper to shame me! In it, he'd written all the details of our time together. Including our address.' She gave Lottie a sharp look. 'I managed to get it off him, then a scuffle broke out. There was a paperweight on his desk and... well, I don't need to tell you the rest. I tore that letter up into pieces and took it with me. Some must have dropped from my hand, which is how *that girl*,' she pointed at Lottie, 'found them. And how I tried to stop you, Lottie Sprigg! It seems that a gunshot or two doesn't scare you off.'

'A gunshot?' said Mrs Moore.

'Yes. Charles and I grew suspicious of Lottie. He'd caught her snooping at a window and listening to his conversation with Lucien. I decided to keep an eye on her. Did you know she travelled all the way to Père Lachaise cemetery with Pierre the delivery boy?'

'No!'

'I followed them in a taxi.'

'Père Lachaise cemetery?' said Madeleine. 'Where Tom and I went?'

'Yes,' said Lottie. 'Pierre and I followed you.'

'Why?'

'Because she enjoys snooping,' said Mrs Lenoir. 'I fired Antoine's revolver into the air just to give you a scare. But it didn't work.'

'So no one was trying to shoot me?' said Madeleine.

'No.'

'But I told you about the gunshots in the cemetery, Mother, and you didn't admit it was you. You lied! Again!'

'It looks like everyone has been doing their fair share of

lying,' said Mrs Moore. 'And it seems to me, Charles, that you tried to protect your mother.'

'I did! I told Lucien to leave and I only wish I could have done more.' The young man dabbed his eyes with a handkerchief. 'Mother didn't deserve this. She made a mistake when she was young.'

'So what now, Commissaire?' said Mrs Moore. 'Although Harriet Lenoir shouldn't have murdered two people, you can see how she was driven to do it.'

The detective took his pipe from his mouth. 'There's a lot to consider,' he said. 'One can't simply take matters into one's own hands in these cases. I shall have to speak with my superiors. But my own personal feeling is that some leniency should be shown.'

Chapter Thirty-Five

'HOW HIGH UP ARE WE?' asked Lottie, peering cautiously at the dizzying view.

'Nearly one thousand feet,' said Pierre.

'I feel like we're up in the clouds.'

'We are, nearly!'

The sun was low on the horizon, casting an orange glow across the sky and over the rooftops, boulevards and parks. The River Seine was a grey, shiny ribbon.

Rosie sniffed at the barrier of the Eiffel Tower's viewing platform, seemingly oblivious to the fact she was so high in the sky.

'Can you see the Arc de Triomphe?' said Pierre, pointing it out. 'And leading off it is the Champs-Élysées. Let's move round so we can see Notre Dame cathedral.'

'How many times have you been up here?' asked Lottie.

'Ten maybe. Or twelve. It might even be twenty!' He grinned.

It was Lottie's last evening in Paris and she couldn't think of a better way to spend it. Mrs Moore had remained adamant she wouldn't climb the Eiffel Tower, but she'd been happy for Pierre to accompany Lottie and Rosie there.

'It's beautiful,' said Lottie, as she watched the orange sky deepen to a red hue. Little lights twinkled in the city below.

'You must come back to Paris one day,' said Pierre. 'I can show you more of the sights.'

'I'd like that.'

'So would I.'

They exchanged a smile, and Lottie was sad she had to leave. 'I have to get back to the hotel,' she said. 'Mrs Moore told me I need to be in bed early because we have a busy few days ahead.'

'Sitting on a train, then a boat? That doesn't sound very busy to me.'

'It is when you're with Mrs Moore.'

IT WAS GETTING dark by the time they'd taken the lift to the bottom of the tower. The call of roosting birds echoed over the river as streaks of purple cloud spread across the western horizon.

Pierre picked up his bicycle and Lottie lifted Rosie into the basket on the front.

'One last bicycle ride,' said Pierre. 'Are you ready?'

THE END

Thank you

Thank you for reading this Lottie Sprigg mystery. I really hope you enjoyed it! Here are a few ways to stay in touch:

- Join my mailing list and receive a FREE short story *Murder in Milan*: marthabond.com/murder-in-milan
- Like my brand new Facebook page: facebook.com/marthabondauthor

Murder in Cairo

Book 3 in the Lottie Sprigg Mystery Series!

Young sleuth, Lottie Sprigg, accompanies her employer to Cairo - a city flushed with excitement after the discovery of Tutankhamun's tomb. But a shadow looms after the untimely death of Lord Carnarvon - could the Pharaoh's Curse be real?

Fears are confirmed when a wealthy hotel guest is poisoned. While some blame the long-dead pharaoh, Lottie's suspicions fall on her fellow guests. They're all up to no good, but can she work out why?

Another murder leaves the Cairo police baffled. Lottie's gathered some clues and thinks she's on the right track. But before she can act, her beloved dog, Rosie, is in danger...

Get your copy: mybook.to/cairomurder

A free Lottie Sprigg mystery

Find out what happens when Lottie, Rosie and Mrs Moore catch the train to Paris in this free mystery *Murder in Milan*!

Lottie and Mrs Moore are travelling from Venice to Paris when their journey is halted at Milan. A passenger has been poisoned and no one can resume their trip until the killer is caught. Trapped in a dismal hotel with her corgi sidekick, Lottie is handed a mysterious suitcase which could land her in trouble...

Events escalate with a second poisoning. Lottie must clear her name and find the killer before the trip is cancelled for good!

Visit my website to claim your free copy:
marthabond.com/murder-in-milan

Or scan the code on the following page:

Also by Martha Bond

Lottie Sprigg Country House Mystery Series:

Murder in the Library
Murder in the Grotto
Murder in the Maze

Writing as Emily Organ:

Augusta Peel Mystery Series:

Death in Soho
Murder in the Air
The Bloomsbury Murder
The Tower Bridge Murder
Death in Westminster

Penny Green Mystery Series:

Limelight
The Rookery

Printed in Great Britain
by Amazon